The Ghost of Alice

The Ghost Of Alice

Christine Vernon

Published by Christine Vernon, 2022.

This is a work of fiction. Similarities to real people, places, or events are entirely coincidental.

THE GHOST OF ALICE

First edition. January 17, 2022.

ISBN: 979-8201811617

Written by Christine Vernon.

Dedication

To the people of the South Strand, Murrells Inlet, and the many guests I have hosted on my Inlet Walking Tours, without whose support this book would not have been possible. Thank you.

Introduction

The following is a historical novel based on actual individuals and one particular family that lived and prospered in the Murrells Inlet, South Carolina area during the days of rice plantations. Although I use the names of the family and their neighbors in this novel, it is a work of pure fiction. Much of the book relies on imagination to create but I have also added some historical facts regarding plantation life. I have fallen in love with certain historical families who once dwelt on the Georgetown County plantations, but there is one particular family who leaves behind a mystery or two. My imagination carries me away to a time from 1800 to 1850. There is a legend that has held me captivated since my moving to the region in 2005. The story of Miss Alice Belin Flagg. I have told her story hundreds of times while performing my ghost and history tour along the saltmarsh on the MarshWalk. This half-mile walk connects a small group of seafood restaurants. The saltmarsh is home to a variety of colorful wildlife. Egrets and blue herons dance through the marsh reeds hunting for small fish while fishermen go in search of shrimp, oysters, flounder and many other inhabitants that the locals and visitors eat on a daily basis. People come from far and wide to our inlet...our reputation as "The Seafood Capital of South Carolina" precedes us. But, we haven't always been a fishing village. Fishing became an important industry from the 1940s till today. Other industries such as hunting and lumber would find their way in the early 1900s. But from Pre-Civil War until the late 1890s rice would be the number one cash crop.

The other water source in our area is the Waccamaw River. The river received its name from the Waccamaw Indian Tribe who still exist today, though not in the same general area. They have only a few acres left many miles west of Murrells Inlet. This was their land. This was their burial ground...their cemetery. They named the area 'Wachasaw', which means the 'place of great weeping'. It would be this name that the Belin/Flagg family would use to name their plantation. I've always wondered why such a sad name. But as I continue my research it does become a fitting title regarding the life of Alice and her family.

The Waccamaw River was the most important element when it came to the life of rice plantation owners. The river is a tidal one, and is important to the growing of rice. Carolina Gold Rice would make the owners in the area very rich... and others exhausted and beaten. Growing rice was the most laborest job in the South. Having to control the river's water levels was intensive as well as dangerous. Many would lose their lives due to injury, infections, snake bites, malaria or just plain exhaustion or heat stroke. Only the strong would survive.

We are entering the years from 1800 to 1850. During this time, many families were settling in Murrells Inlet (formerly called 'Murrays' Inlet and acquiring the 'Murrells' Inlet name around 1914). Charleston is only a 2 hour drive south but in 1800 it could take as many as 2-3 days to reach the city. There were many families who were already established as planters such as the Al(l)stons, LaBruce, Ward, Fraser and others, along with the Belin and Flagg families. Belin/Flaggs would find their fortunes along the Waccamaw River from Sandy Island towards the inlet. Some of the wealthiest families in all of South Carolina lived here in Murrells Inlet. It was the most prosperous time for the Belins and Flaggs but also, one of the saddest. Not only is this book about the trials of plantation life, especially for ladies of the period, it is also a love story. But with most love stories comes heartbreak.

I hope you enjoy this work of fiction. I have always loved a good mystery and I hope you do too.

I do ask one favor of everyone who reads this story of Alice Flagg. She is at peace. And, I believe, would like to stay at peace. Alice Flagg is not buried beneath the stone at All Saints but many people call upon her there. So you may think you are calling upon her spirit at her memorial stone, but you may just awaken another. And this spirit may take a fancy to you and follow you home.

I believe Alice wishes to be at her beloved Hermitage where hopefully one day, she will find her ring.

Chapter One

"Hurry...it's getting dark already!"

Three young girls nervously creep towards an old sign swinging in a gentle breeze above an old iron gate. It reads All Saints Cemetery in faded letters. The girls stand in front of the gate, but none will touch it. They each pause and look at each other, just waiting to see who will touch the cold black metal first. Lynn rolls her eyes and pushes the gate forward. The squeaking of the old iron makes their skin crawl. Hoping they didn't attract attention, Lynn and her friends, Jan and Joyce scurry into the cemetery. They begin their journey through the graveyard, dodging crooked headstones along the way. Ancient oak tree branches reach out across the evening sky. Spanish moss dripping from their limbs. Suddenly, Jan trips over a small marker and collapses on a huge marble slab. Candles and a lighter fall from her purse.

"God, you were always the clumsy one," whispers Lynn. " I hope you didn't break anything?"

"Do we have to do this at night? I mean, won't this work in the daytime too?" asks Joyce.

Lynn turns swiftly around and shakes her head. "Y'all said you wanted to do this, so let's do this!"

As Jan brushes herself off all three girls look down. They found what they were looking for. The stone is time worn but the name upon it was still visible...Alice.

"Now what?" questions Joyce.

Lynn grabs the candles and hands one to each of her friends and lights them. The flames wave at the girls as if to say goodbye. She asks Jan for the last item for their ritual. A ring. Jan reaches into her jeans pocket and pulls out a gold band and hands it to Lynn. Lynn slides the ring on her left index finger. She has her friends stand on either side of the stone. Lynn walks to the head of the stone then takes a couple steps towards the right. A path had been previously etched into the earth around the grave. It looked like many had been here before wondering the same thing as these three ladies. Will this work? Will we see her?

Lynn takes another step to the right, then another. The girls watch her carefully. Suddenly, Joyce sees something in the grove of trees nearby. Without saying a word she points in the direction of what seems to be a small, white orb of light dancing through the brush. Jan looks and lets out a small gasp. She grabs Lynn by her shirt. All three are now looking towards this mysterious light coming closer towards them. They begin to feel the breeze becoming colder and colder. The moss swaying to and fro in unison, as if keeping time like a conductor's metrodome. They can hear the breaking of branches ...something is coming their way. The light begins to grow larger, almost blinding. They are frozen in fear. None can move nor say a sound. Then finally a voice is heard calling out from the light towards the ladies.

"Hey...what are you kids doing out here!?"

All three scream at once, drop their candles and run towards the iron gate. The figure chases after them but they have found their way back to the cemetery exit and without looking back, continue to scream and run down the darkened street.

"Damn kids. They always gotta mess with this place. Why can't they just leave her in peace?'

Then, the uniformed officer walks back towards his cruiser to make out his report. This isn't the first time this has happened and he knows it's not the last. He sits in the front seat of his vehicle and shakes his head. As he begins his report he does not realize the sound of crying coming from inside the cemetery. Just soft whimpers at first. Then the faint, tiny whisper of the words, "Where is the Hermitage? Where is my ring?"

Chapter Two

"It's a girl!"

Margaret Belin Flagg is in her early 30's. Her soulful brown eyes are full of tears and her long chestnut hair is full of sweat. She gazes up at her husband, Dr. Ebenezer Flagg. She has been waiting and worrying about this moment for some time. It is November of 1833. This is her 10th and probably the last child she will give birth to. Her body was strong but her heart was weak. Not with disease, but with sorrow. She had given birth 10 months earlier, but the baby boy was 2 months premature and would not last the day.

Her mind wanders back to the loss of her first daughter. It had been seven years since she lost Gertrude. The baby did not make it to her first birthday. Just two years prior to losing her baby girl, her son, Walter died before his first birthday as well. Even though this was not uncommon for childbearing women of that era, it was still nonetheless heartbreaking each and every time. She would again be blessed with a son, Charles who would spend the majority of his years in military school and away from the plantation.

But it was the year 1822 that shattered her and her husband's lives with the deaths of two sons, Edward and Allard Jr. Edward just made it to his 3rd birthday while Allard Jr. barely his second. It seemed each time they were blessed with a child, God would take one away. She had just given birth to her husband's namesake, Eben when she buried her two sons and she was frightened that God would take this child away, too. But, Margaret would give birth to a healthy son a year later. They would name him Allard ll in remembrance of the son she just lost. And as Allard ll would grow strong, his mother would grow more controlling over his every move. With every cough or fever, Margaret would panic. With each pregnancy, more tears would fall. She would live in fear with each pregnancy. Maybe it was best to distance herself. Maybe if she did not love them so much her heart would not break. But, instead, her anxiety would grow and she would not let the remainder of her children out of her sight. If she were not there to protect them from harm at every moment, she may lose another to the angel of death.

Margaret looks down at her precious infant. She was so grateful to have a girl again. And she vowed that nothing would happen to this child. She had become wary of every little sniffle or cough from her children. She watched them as closely as a mother bear over her cubs. Nothing was going to happen to this child, her baby girl. Absolutely nothing.

Dr. Eben (as his friends called him), and his wife Margaret loved having a large family. Their life in Charleston is a good one financially. They have been blessed with wealth from both sides of the family. Both had found their financial stability from plantations. They had bought land in an area called Murrells Inlet which is just north of Charleston. Here they are able to acquire more wealth to ensure a comfortable existance. It was from a particular rice called Carolina Gold that made many of the Waccamaw Neck area from Charleston to Murrells Inlet extremely rich. The Waccamaw River was a source of rich earth and fresh water that was the best for growing rice. But, it was their slaves that knew how to grow and harvest it. They had come from an area of Africa called Gola and their ancestors were very astute at mastering the land and water. But, they are now brought to a new land filled with diseases such as yellow fever, malaria and typhoid. Poisonous snakes like water moccasin and copperhead were always hiding beneath stones and stumps. Alligators would slowly swim with stealth and power to overtake their victims if they happen to be too close to the water's edge.

Most plantation families would travel north to escape the heat and humidity of summer. On occasion, the Flaggs and Belins would spend the hot summers in Charleston or near the ocean at a smaller home. Their main house near the Waccamaw River in Murrells Inlet was still going through construction, but Reverend James Belin, Margaret's brother, had a modest home nearby and some members of the family would stay there to oversee their plantations. But during the holiday season from November until January, Margaret and her family will stay in Charleston. Once Margaret is feeling better in early spring, the family will head back to Murrells Inlet with their new baby girl, Alice. And Margaret will make sure that Alice will have the best of everything.

The Belin family had lived in Murrells Inlet since 1800. James Belin knew the land there was perfect for growing rice along with sweet potatoes, squash, and cotton that would be grown further west of the river. But, they were mostly interested in rice production. So, Margaret's father, James Allard Belin bought a plantation from one of the wealthy Allston's whose family thrived in the growing of rice. The name of the plantation was Wachesaw. He had heard the name from the people of the area that Wachesaw may mean happy hunting ground, but others would know the true meaning of the word. It was the Waccamaw Indian Tribe that named this area Wachesaw...and for good reason. Not only did the tribe live here near the fresh water of the river and create salt from the brine of the inlet, but they used this land for one specific purpose. To bury their dead. Burial mounds had been found throughout the area when Europeans first came upon these shores. Many of the mounds had multiple skeletons found inside. So the tribal people named the area Wachesaw... 'the place of great weeping.' It would be a sad decision to name this plantation after an Indian graveyard. Many hoped the name would not come back to haunt them or bring them bad luck.

James Allard Belin Sr decided to send his son James Lynch Belin to run his affairs and the duties entailed with the management of the plantation. James Lynch did not want to be the owner of a plantation. His idea of life was far from scribbling in accounting ledgers and managing slaves. But, it was his father's will and he was a dutiful son. So, when he was old enough, he left for Murrells Inlet to run his father's estate.

In time, all would go well at Wachesaw. Sweet potatoes, squash, corn and other vegetables would be key in keeping the family well fed. And, of course, rice would be what made men wealthy. The wealthiest people in all the pre-Civil War South lived in Murrells Inlet. These families would build the most palatial homes in Charleston. Money was no object. But a man's wealth didn't always come from the earth or water. It came from his other commodity - slaves.

In time James Lynch Belin would decide that the life of overseer and accountant would not be for him. He would receive a higher calling. That of a Methodist minister. His family belonged to the local All Saints Episcopal Church. But a new religion was making its way through the region. Methodism. Belin had seen the bishops preaching around the area and he liked what he heard. So, he approached the bishops and asked to become a minister. At first, the church rejected his request. Belin was confused and asked for a reason for their denial. They explained that Belin was a slave owner. Owning slaves was against doctrine, although the ministers did not push the agenda too harshly to other slave owners. They were calmly trying to make their way into southern society. They needed a foot hold so they could start their own church. So Belin gave them an ultimatum. He decided to give up the majority of his land, property and slaves to his nephew, Allard ll. Until he is old enough to take over the responsibilities, his sister Margaret will run his plantation. James would keep one hundred acres for himself. He would name it Cedar Hill. If he were to be made a

Methodist minister, he would decree in his last will and testament that his 100 acres would go to the church. And they agreed...of course.

James Lynch Belin would become the local Reverend of the Methodist Church and would begin a mission. Not only to help the spiritual needs of the plantation owners and their families, but also help the slaves themselves. He would offer to teach them about the bible. To teach a slave was a dangerous thing. It was against the law to teach slaves. However, through Reverend Belin's tenaciousness and love for all mankind and the word of the God, he would slowly be accepted into the fold of plantation society.

The Flaggs and Belins had been close for many years, mainly by marriage, so managing a plantation together with family from both sides only made the family stronger. Many of the Flaggs were doctors. It was common to have at least one physician in each plantation family, but there were quite a few in the Flagg family. And to have a man of the cloth would be an added bonus, even though the religion he was associated with had a tendency to look down upon slavery. But, James was a good hearted man and Margaret was hoping that in these more modern days of medicine and having a Man of God in their home,the chances of her children making it into adulthood would increase.

Margaret was exhausted after the birth of her baby girl and needed desperately to rest. She is only 32 years old and has lost so much. Four of ten children, so far. She was always reliant on her wet nurses and house servants to help take care of the children, especially when they were sick. If Margaret heard just a simple cough or sneeze, she would call out to her maid to bring the camphor,opium and laudanum. Summer was also a serious time for diseases like swamp or country fever. For this, purging or bleeding with leeches would be the common medical practice. But Margaret has come to rely on her husband, Eben when it came to the bloodletting.

Margaret spent much of her time running the household and watching her children and would keep an eye especially on her son,

Allard ll. He is only ten years old, but she knew that was a milestone. Children during her time would succumb to fevers often. Infections were very prevalent and took many lives of both slaves and plantation families. For a child to make it this far was considered a blessing. She has watched her other son, Eben Belin Jr, only 11 years old at this time, become very self-sufficient and is always by his father's side. She knows he will become a doctor, just like his father. Her other son Arthur, a very mischievous 5 year old, is also becoming more like his father each day. He is trying to escape his mother's apron strings, but Margaret pulls them as tight as she can. She must. He is still at an age of uncertainty as to whether he will see his next birthday. When her son, Walter died in 1831, she was full of anxiety and often melancholy. When she found herself with child in '32, she knew this child would pass away as well. She tried to explain this to her doctor/husband, but he would repeatedly tell her that everything would be just fine. But,she could feel this pregnancy was different. So when this tiny, fragile boy passed before her 8th month, Margaret was not so sure she wanted another child. How could she? How could she bury another child and her broken heart into another grave?

But, she could not refuse the role of wife. She had a duty to her husband. A duty to bear children and leave a legacy for them. This was her station in life. This was the role of wives. Especially plantation wives. It is the job of every wife on every plantation to do as her husband instructs. She must also manage the household and the slaves. But in doing so she too has become a kind of slave herself.

The house servants would be incredibly important to Margaret right now. Margaret was in no shape to manage anything after Alice's birth. Her servant, Martha would be by her side day and night if need be. Martha was also with child and soon she would have her own little girl. But, Martha was not happy. Oh, she looked forward to seeing her first born, but not here. Not this way. But, as a house servant, she was able to eat better than most who worked the fields. She was also less likely to become injured or suffer from dehydration working the fields under horrid conditions. Somehow she knew her pregnancy would be a healthy one...at least she hoped so.

Martha had a good husband. He was also a house servant, the driver for the family. It was a big responsibility and not to be taken lightly. He would be on call day and night for the family. He was even given a powerful name ...Hurricane. He was given that name because he had been born during a tremendous sea surge that took many lives. He was quite large, nearly 10 lbs at birth. He grew up strong and could row a boat faster than any man. He was 6 feet tall and one of the strongest field hands the family owned. He was quite an asset. But he was also an intelligent man and had worked hard each day to make his quota. Each slave was given a quota, a schedule they had to follow every day. Normally, a male with his strength should have remained in the fields. But, it was fate that would bring Hurricane and Martha together not only as house servants, but husband and wife.

It was a few years after Margaret had lost her two boys in 1822 that she nearly lost Allard ll. Margaret and the family were living with Reverend Belin at this time. She was feeling very melancholy that day. It was the anniversary of her son Edward's death and in her depressive state of mind she had taken her eyes off Allard ll. She sat and stared out the drawing room window towards the field next to the home, her eyes red and swollen from her tears. The family often stayed at Reverend Belin's house by the marsh in cooler weather. Allard woke up from his nap and decided to go to the marsh behind the house. It was low tide and the mud was fragrant and thick. He saw a small fish that had been trapped in a muddy puddle of water. It was just within reach of his tiny hands. Allard reached out as far as he could but would fall over the slippery edge. He fell head first into the mire of the puddle. While trying to catch his breath he instead was inhaling the mud into his lungs. With each little breath, the mud would creep further into his throat, choking him.

At that same time, Hurricane was coming to report to Dr. Eben regarding the ricebirds that were going for the seed in the fields. Most times the family didn't plant in April due to flocks of birds devouring every seed, but the family had a late start due to the cold winter. As Hurricane walked toward the home, he heard splashing. Thinking it was a good size flounder or a heron that had gotten caught in the marsh reeds, he walked over and saw little Allard struggling in the pluff mud. But with each movement, the mud became more like quicksand and it was pulling the child under. Hurricane ran as fast as he could to the water's edge and with all his might pulled the child up with one hand. He quickly rushed into the home. Finding a basin of water in the kitchen he began to wash the child's mouth out so the little one could catch his breath. Poor Allard was coughing up mud and phlegm but still was unable to breath. Hurricane put the child over his knee and patted him on his back over and over. Hurricane hoped this would make it easier for Allard to cough up the mud out of his mouth.

Margaret heard the coughing and began to run through the household calling out to Allard. She then finds Hurricane beating on the child and instantly thinks the worst. She picks up a large ladle and proceeds to hit Hurricane. He continues to pat the child on the back...he is more concerned about the child than he is about the pain from the beating. Dr. Eben hears the commotion from his office and rushes into the kitchen to find his wife hysterically crying and trying to pull Allard away from Hurricane. When Hurricane sees his master walking towards him, he drops to his knees and he hands his son over to him. Dr. Eben immediately sees what has happened to his son. He snatches Allard from Hurricane's hands and continues to wash out the child's mouth. Hurricane stays on the ground and waits for further punishment. But, it does not come. Dr. Eben is able to remove what was left of the mud and Allard takes a huge breath and begins to cry. Margaret grabs her son and cradles him. It is a minute later that both the doctor and his wife see Hurricane still on his knees on the ground.

Eben questions him and Hurricane recalls the story of finding the boy in the marsh.

Margaret, who rarely shows any sign of emotion in front of her staff, falls to her knees. She looks Hurricane in the eyes and praises him for his quick thinking and saving her son's life. Eben pulls his wife up from the kitchen floor, tells her to wash the child and put him to bed. Margaret takes the child into the next room. Dr. Eben pulls Hurricane aside and offers his hand. Hurricane is reluctant to shake. It is not the place of a slave to touch his master. Eben reaches out once more and nods his head. Hurricane smiles softly, nods his head and takes the doctor's hand. It would be from then on that Hurricane would work at the house. Margaret would spend her days knowing that she could rely on him. From that day on, Hurricane and Martha would work together under the Belin/Flagg's roof. And would eventually be given permission by the Flaggs to have a family of their own.

The family thought it would be a good match, and gave permission for the two to marry. Their marriage, of course, is not looked upon as legal in the South. It only meant they were given permission to start a family. Although Martha was very happy to have Hurricane as her mate, one thing frightened her. There was always something that loomed over Martha's head. That one day, their family would be torn apart. She had seen it happen many times before. If an owner died, slaves were sold off to pay their debt. Or, if a servant was dishonest or disobeyed they would find themselves being sold to a plantation many miles away. Martha has been a valuable asset to Margaret and the children. But, in order to keep her new family together, she would have to work even harder. Her due date was coming close and it made her wonder if this would change the relationship she had with her owner. Would the child be healthy? Would it be a hindrance? Would she make it through the birth? Her... and the child?

But now was not the time to think about this. She had work to do. There was Ms. Margaret to be thinking about during her time of need.

And, to take care of the sweet, new baby girl Alice that has just come into this world. She would be well taken care of. Martha would make sure of that.

Margaret turns towards Martha holding Alice up in her arms.

"Martha, please take the child and set her down, I need to rest."

Martha smiles sweetly and gazes at the baby. She was a tiny thing. Fragile. Like some of the others. Her eyes were open and fixated on Martha. She does as she is told and takes the child to another room. Margaret is frail and needs desperately to sleep. She must regain her strength quickly. There was much to do on the plantation. Plus, she must attend to her other children who were behind on their education. She shakes her head, trying to clear out these overwhelming thoughts. She'll figure out everything in the morning, after a good night's sleep.

Martha places Alice in a small bassinet. The child seems just as exhausted as her mother and goes to sleep quickly. Martha hopes that's a good sign. But, sometimes it's the babies that cry the hardest and the loudest who are the healthiest. Alice's siblings weren't as quiet when they were babes and are still here. Martha watches over the child and says a little prayer.

"Lawd, watch ober dis chile 'n gib her strength."

Chapter Three

The weather hasn't been cooperating lately. As Spring grows into Summer, the heat has become unbearable. Along with the humidity. It is all but impossible to breathe let alone work out in the fields. But, this is a very important time in the growing season. The last full moon's tides along with a small gale caused some intense moments. The rice fields stand about two and one-half feet above the level of the river. The river is tidal and perfect for growing rice. When the river waters rise, the floodgates (called trunks) are raised up and the fresh water works its way into the rice fields. But,when there is a sudden surge of water, all the trunks must be opened at once otherwise the river will flood other areas. Growing rice was a tidal business. The family was at the mercy of God and Mother Nature and all must trust in He and She. If the other fields of corn and squash become flooded, they will have lost months of time and money.

And during these months of humidity and un-godly heat there is also the threat of disease. Many plantation families leave the Waccamaw River area and return to their palaces in Charleston or head further north past the Mason -Dixon line. Others will go towards the west to the mountains near Tennessee to break away from the climate. But, the doctors and husbands will remain to make sure the tedious work is accomplished. Country fever/swamp fever (also known as malaria) was rampant. Especially by the river side. This is why most families also built smaller, summer plantation homes by the inlet or beach. With their shutters wide open, they could catch some relief from the ocean winds. Margaret and the family stay with Reverend

Belin on occasion to escape the heat. One day they will build their own retreat by the marshy inlet.

Unfortunately, Margaret cannot leave the area just yet to take her little girl Alice back to Charleston. The baby has croup and has become colicky. Her tiny throat was closing up and her cough was raspy. Her husband Eben, was currently in Charleston so it was up to her to use her know-how. She had been through this before with Edward who died very young. Her panic was about to begin again at the thought of losing another child.

She had used rosemary and hyssop before but added a bit of sugar to the mix so it would be palatable to a baby. Later, she may try syrup of poppies (opium) to soothe Alice so she may finally fall to sleep. The constant cough and wheezing was becoming repetitive and causing anxiety to build up in Margaret. She was needing Martha now more than ever. But Martha was busy giving birth to her own child.

Martha was going through a painful time herself. She had been in labor for hours, but was having difficulty with delivering her child. One of the other servants, Cloie was patting her forehead down with a wet cloth while her mother Libby, was down on her knees at the end of Martha's bed, coaching her on. They found a small switch for Martha to bite down on each time the pain was too much. Libby tells Martha to push again, but suddenly holds her hand up to stop her. The baby is breaching. This was more serious than they had expected. There was nothing else to do but take the child quickly. One more push and Libby takes the child by her ankles. Martha has no strength left but Libby is able to pull the child towards her. The child has not taken her first breath yet. The umbilical cord is still around her neck. Libby quickly unravels the cord and lowers the baby into a small bucket of water. That was just the thing to get the infant to gasp, and then let out a strong cry. She takes some twine,ties off and cuts the cord. Finding a shawl, she wraps the crying baby and places it onto Martha's breast.

Libby falls back down on her knees, holding her hands above her head and calls out, "Et be a gurl...an'a lucky one et dat, tenk Gawd! Praise be de Lawd 'n Mary, too!"

Martha's dark set brown eyes are full of tears. She slowly caresses her newborn's head. Now she knows what to name her little one. Mary. She knows Hurricane was hoping for a boy, but this little girl would have to do. Martha had also hoped for a son. A son could fend for himself. He could work hard to feed the household. But a girl? In this day and age on the plantations, some servant girls would be at the mercy of their owners. And, if their owner was not a good Christian man, a young slave girl would have to do his bidding. But, Martha wasn't too concerned in that regard. Dr. Eben was a God fearing man. He had never made Martha uncomfortable in the house where she worked. But wasn't sure about any other slave. Nor did Reverend Belin who was extremely charitable and giving to her and her people. But, that didn't mean some of the other workers on the plantation wouldn't keep their hands off a young, pretty girl. Women were at the bottom of the totem pole. They were always needed, but rarely appreciated.

Word reaches the ears of Margaret while she is staying with her brother at his inlet home about the birth of Martha's child. But, she is unable to visit Martha at the driver's shack to see if she and the baby are well. She only hopes Martha can make it back to the summer house to fulfill her duties. It has become overwhelming for Margaret and she is having to give responsibility to other house servants during this anxious time.

Margaret sends word to her brother, James to come and say a prayer for poor Alice. She has done all she can think of to help her baby girl. The only recipe that soothes the child in the afternoon is a concoction of sherry and water to help her sleep.

When the Reverend arrives, he knows what he must do. He has been through this before with his nephews many years ago. He feels powerless. He feels his prayers were not answered before. But, he is determined to fight for his niece. This one is special. It is the last of the line. He and his own wife, Elizabeth could not bear children and it was yellow fever that took her poor soul away. Now, his new bride of two years Charlotte, has not conceived a child yet. So he has looked upon his sister's children as his own. It will be his mission to make sure Alice is watched over. His affection for his sister's children is like that of any proud parent. He dotes on his nephews and spends many hours teaching them the bible. He not only teaches his own family but the slaves at Wachesaw, too. He knows that the power of God is in all beings, including his servants. He has fought long and hard to establish himself and his congregation in the Waccamaw Neck region. Many dismiss his mission to the slaves that he has dedicated himself to. He established the mission when he was first ordained a minister and believed it would help in keeping both owner and slave honest.

James taps gently on the parlor door just beside Margaret's bedroom. She is weary; her hair has not been combed. Dark shadows are etched beneath her dark brown eyes. She is paler than usual. She is rocking in her favorite rocking chair and nods to James to come in. James quietly enters and smiles softly at Alice cradled in Margaret's arms. Margaret lifts her index finger to her lips. Alice has finally gone to sleep and Margaret is afraid if she stops rocking, Alice will wake up. James lifts his hand over Alice. He slowly makes the sign of the cross and whispers to himself. Alice stirs but remains asleep. Both Margaret and James hold their breath but she remains calm. Margaret bows her head along with James and repeats the blessing to herself. She has always had faith in God, but feels she is losing hope. James finishes his prayer and turns to Margaret. He places his hand on her head. She pulls away. She would rather that the blessing be completely for Alice's sake. He shakes his head and places his hand on her head again. He mouths the words...'*ye need this as much as she.*' Margaret smiles at her brother and bows her head, accepting his gift. She needs all the strength she can get.

James leaves the room quietly and walks behind his home towards the inlet. It feels good to have his family staying here but knows once Alice is well enough, the family will depart for Charleston or further north where the weather is healthier and cooler. Margaret prefers to stay further north or in the mountains during the late Spring and through the Summer months. The oppressive heat and humidity is overwhelming for all, but especially for women and children. Margaret panics during this season. Yellow fever is prevalent during this time and families are leaving in droves. Dr. Eben has many good people working the fields and watching over daily affairs. But he usually stays in Charleston to keep up his medical practice or sometimes he is called to Georgetown, another river town directly between Murrells Inlet and Charleston. Doctors are in very high demand during the summer growing season. So are men of the cloth. This time of year puts all manner of beast and man to the test. The health of many depend on these men of both science and religion.

Belin looks out over the waters brimming with fish and all manner of wildlife. He pauses by an oak tree and watches as tiny mullets swim in schools by the hundreds causing rippling pools as they head out with the tide. So far, the weather has been good for planting. He may be a minister, but he is still responsible for the well-being of his family and that includes their stomachs.

He spies his nephew, Allard walking along the sandy shore. Allard is ten years old and is one of his favorites. Belin is aware a person should never admit to having a favorite child, but Allard is the closest thing to a son he thinks he will ever have. And Alice...his daughter. His other nephews, Arthur and Eben are very close to their father and aren't the best when it comes to their religious studies. But Allard, James foretells, will be the one to take over and do great things when he is grown.

Belin approaches Allard. "Are you looking forward to being released from your summer imprisonment and returning to the north or has your mother's decision to spend these ghastly months in Charleston prevailed?"

Allard shakes his head. "I have not heard. I do hope we will go back to the north again. Massachusetts is much more to my liking, but I will miss my mare."

Belin pats his nephew on the head. "I too, wish nothing more but to escape this inferno, but duty and God calls. It would be nice to see our family in Massachusetts but your mother may be too fatigued to make the long voyage. Take care that you and your siblings do not disturb your mother. She has exhausted herself."

Allard nods his head and leaves to find his brothers. He imagines they are by the stables. The stables have a collection of animals and the boys' favorite is an old marsh-tack mare. All three boys can ride this huge animal at once, but it is mainly used in the fields along with other horses. Cattle roam freely along with an assortment of hens and of course, an ornery rooster.

Their land is well over 900 acres of both fields of corn, squash and greens along with pine forest and the occasional oak and cedar tree. The only way the plantation owners know their boundary lines is by the placement of certain trees. There are other markers that divide the different homesteads as well. The children know not to pass the long stretch of burial mounds located on their land. The graves are the only remnants of the Waccamaw Tribe that once lived and died in the region. The slaves know to keep their distance from these graves, also. A family could be cursed if they did not pay their respects by placing some food or tobacco near the site. Many of the slaves brought their own haints and haunts with them from Africa. They certainly did not wish to upset the spirits of this land.

There is also another creature that the children and adults need to watch out for as well. Alligators. This is still wetlands throughout the plantations. Although it is perfect for growing rice, it is also perfect for growing gators. These creatures lurk just under the muddy river water.

They may look slow but they are dangerous and quick to kill. They have taken a slave not too long ago. The unfortunate soul was fishing for his family's dinner when the event occurred. After that, Margaret made sure the boys would be watched at all times when they went down to the river. But on occasion, they would slip away from their babysitters.

Allard makes his way to the stables but decides to take a short cut through the slave shacks. There are nearly 80 slaves on this plantation and all live in a tiny community of cabins. Sometimes upwards of 10 people crammed into one building. There are two rows of houses with a courtyard in between. At the end of the row is the driver's hut. This is where Hurricane and Martha live. And, now their baby girl, Mary.

Allard owes his life to Hurricane and they have become fast friends. He can tell Hurricane anything...well,almost. He knows that Hurricane must report to Margaret if he sees anything go astray, and that goes for any of her boys. But, there are times when he can go for just some friendly advice. His father, Eben, is away quite often. He travels from plantation to plantation to heal the sick. It is an exhausting profession. And, will eventually take its toll.

As Allard gets close to the hut, he can hear the cries of a baby. He knows Martha has had a child and doesn't want to disturb her, so he peeks through the window. He sees Martha cradling her infant in her arms. He suddenly drops down out of sight. He is not supposed to be in the area so close to dark and doesn't want to be seen. So he runs off to the stables to find his brothers and bring them home for dinner.

The trail takes him near the tar kiln. The smell of turpentine and burning peat fills his lungs. He holds his breath and dashes towards the stables. The turpentine is in high demand these days for marine vessels. But, the family was not interested in acquiring a profit. This would only be for their personal use. The smoke from the peat hurts his lungs. He has had some trouble with his breath ever since his incident in the inlet. He continues on his journey to seek his brothers. He is famished. Although he knows the meal will probably consist of fish and rice again, he will still eat his fill.

Chapter Four

It was a happy occasion this 14th of January 1838. It is Dr. Eben's 43rd birthday and the family is getting ready to celebrate at the main house by the river. His 3 sons and his 4 year old daughter, Alice are creating gifts for their father. Alice has drawn a picture of her father in pen and ink. She is actually starting to show a talent for the arts and Margaret is pleased to see her shy youngest child develop her skills. It would still be a few more years before Alice would be sent away to boarding school in Charleston. There she will be taught the arts as well as her place in society.

But, for now she is always beside her mother's or her Uncle James' side. She loves the stories her uncle teaches from his well-worn Bible that he carries on a constant basis. She has found a liking for the stories of the Bible. She is fascinated by the tale of Noah and his Ark. She has an empathic love for the creatures of the inlet and the plantation. When Margaret takes her down to the inlet creek by her brother's home, she sits in wonder of the wildlife. Herons cautiously stalk their fish dinner while snowy egrets and noisy gulls fly by. All manner of God's creatures crawling along the shoreline neither scare nor upset her. She enjoys watching tiny lizards crawl from one marsh reed to the next, bobbing their heads in a type of courtship in search of a mate. Her little heart fills with joy in the winter because she knows they will be staying in Murrells Inlet until the harsh summer heat begins. She does not like to leave her inlet oasis. At this young age, she has already found her forever home. She doesn't like to travel so often. She complains of stomach aches whenever they leave for Charleston or to journey up north. She is content to stay here forever by her magical marsh.

Darkness is falling and Margaret grows concerned. She knows her husband had a long way to travel from Charleston and the previous day's weather was not good. A steady, cold sleet had blanketed the trails and roadways. It's unusually cold this year and Eben may have stopped in Georgetown to wait out the storm. She knew he had a dear friend who owns Friendsfield plantation and must have sought shelter with him and his family. It would not be the first time he did this.

Margaret calls the children to dinner. The children scamper into the room and into their usual seats. Martha enters the room from the kitchen with a cistern filled with hot soup and begins to fill Margaret's bowl first. She is not alone. Her little girl, Mary, is with her. Mary is also Alice's age and the two have become very close. They consider themselves sisters. Alice is taunted daily by her brothers' relentless teasing, especially by Allard. Mary is the only other girl her age for miles and they share a special bond.

Mary peeks her tiny little head around the kitchen door. She must remain quiet or she and her mother would be in trouble. Alice is the last to make it to the table and notices Mary by the door. She smiles and waves. She softly says the words, "Hello, Sista".

Mary waves back, cups her hands to her mouth and whispers 'hello sista' back. The family has taken to calling Mary 'Sista' on Alices' recommendation.

Martha turns her head and grimisses at her daughter. Sista quickly ducks back through the door. Margaret gives a stern look towards Alice. Alice hangs her head to overt her mother's gaze. Both Margaret and Martha turn to look at each other. Martha suddenly hangs her head and apologizes to her mistress. Margaret gently shakes her head and tells Martha to continue to fill the children's bowls. Martha does as she is told and backs away from the table. She will stand by the kitchen door and wait for further instructions.

"Who will say grace tonight?" Margaret asks.

Alice raises her hand. "May I, mother?"

Margaret nods yes and waits for Alice's blessing.

"Dearest Lord, we thank you for what we are about to receive. And, please bless father on his birthday. Amen"

The family recites 'Amen' in unison and begins to eat.

There is a strong wind approaching from the East off the ocean. The sun is setting and Dr. Eben feels he is unable to continue his trip to Murrells Inlet this night. He had just passed his friend's home and the wind had picked up. He must turn his carriage around and go back for shelter. He is only a mile or so from his friend's home. Hopefully he is there and will take him in. Dr. Eben pulls on the reins. As his horse turns one way, his carriage continues to slide sideways. It gets stuck in the mud just off the side of the roadway. The temperature is dropping and he is unable to pull his carriage out. The mud is quickly freezing and trapping his escape. The man is tired from his hectic schedule and knows if he stays here, he could succumb to the cold and sleet. He elects to unhitch his horse and ride bareback to his friend's home.

Dr. Eben takes the harness off and lifts himself onto his horse. The wind and sleet nearly blind him, but he is certain he can find his way to shelter. Along with the sleet, a slow moving fog moves in over the marsh. Slowly, Dr. Eben and his mare ride into it and disappear from view.

Margaret asks Martha to put the children to bed. The weather has become blustery and Margaret is hoping that her husband has stayed overnight in Georgetown. When the children are under the covers, Margaret visits each one to wish them good night. Margaret can hear Alice whimpering under her covers. She sits down on the edge of the bed and pulls the blanket down. Alice wipes the tears from her eyes and sniffles.

"What is wrong, child?" Margaret asks. But, she already knows why her baby girl is so sad.

"Where is father? I wanted to give him his present but he did not come."

"Do not worry, little one. Your father is a man of common sense and sought shelter with a friend. He will be here on the morrow."

Margaret tucks the blanket up under Alice's chin and kisses her cheek. One of Alice's tears drips onto her lips. She can taste her daughter's tears and hope all of them will be dried by morning.

Margaret drags herself to her bed chamber. Martha is there to assist her into her bed clothes.

"No Martha, I will not sleep tonight. Do not worry yourself over my circumstances. You may leave."

"Yessum, 'mam." answers Martha.

Margaret walks across her chamber and sits in her rocker. This is where she has spent most of her nights... sitting, rocking, pondering, and crying.

The next morning arrives and the weather has broken. The skies are cloudy but the sleet and wind have subsided. Margaret wakes with the morning light and realizes she has fallen asleep in her rocker again. She moves across the hall and peers into her husband's bedroom. He is not there. His bed linens have not been disturbed. She runs down the hall and to the main parlor. Not there. His office. No one. She hears voices in the kitchen and runs into the room. It is only Martha and Sista starting their morning chores.

"Have you seen Dr Eben?" Margaret asks.

"Nah 'mam. No un' up yet."

Margaret begins to feel weak in her knees. She slips onto a chair and puts her head in her hands. She has an awful feeling. A terrible, gnawing feeling that Eben may not have stayed in Georgetown. She feels a pain rip through her heart. She clutches her chest and slowly stands. She turns and heads back to her chamber and waits for word of her husband.

Martha continues with her chores. She is making biscuits and gravy for the children. She knows her mistress is worried about Dr. Eben, and so she begins to make a tray of food to take to her.

Alice has heard her mother's footsteps and comes through the kitchen door. She looks around and sees Martha and Sista baking. Martha knows this will be a difficult day, so she asks Sista to stay with Alice in the kitchen while she takes a tray up to Margaret.

Alice walks over to Sista. "Have you seen my father?"

Sista answers by shaking her head no while stuffing a biscuit in her mouth.

Alice shakes her head with a confused look on her face."I saw him last night. He came to my room. I showed him my picture. He liked it, but did not take it?"

Martha overhears Alice's story from the hall and quickly runs back to the kitchen.

"Wachu mean ya see 'em?" asked Martha.

"I saw my father, but he wouldn't talk to me. Is he mad?"

Martha was frozen. She knew Dr. Eben had not come home last night. No one but she and Sista had entered the home this morning.

"Chile, ya go back to y'alls room."

Alice smiles at Sista and goes back down the hall.

Martha can't bring herself to tell Margaret what she had just heard. She figures the child had a dream and that was all there was to it. There was no need to upset Margaret over this. But, deep down Martha knew it was bad news for the family. For all of them.

Margaret cannot eat a bite of food. She leaves the tray by her dresser in her room. It will be a very long day for her. She determines that if Eben left his friend's home at sunrise, he would be home by supper. So, she must pull herself together and get ready for the day. It would be important to continue with the children's schooling and keep everyone's minds off their father's absence.

But, the hours tick by and by nightfall there is still no sign of Dr. Eben. Margaret sends one of the servants to Reverend Belin's house with news that Dr. Eben has not come home. Once James hears this, he saddles his horse and rides towards the main house.

James approaches the home and finds Margaret alone in the main parlor. She has sent the children upstairs to prepare for bed. It is dark and too late to start any kind of search for the doctor. James agrees that at dawn he and Hurricane will go look for Eben.

At daybreak, Hurricane prepares the horses and carriage for he and Reverend Belin's journey. They are hoping to meet the doctor along the road. It is still misty and damp and both look forward to finding the doctor and coming home. It will take hours to reach Georgetown due to the muddy conditions.

Hours and hours have passed and Margaret becomes concerned. Again, the day has turned to night and there is no word from James or Eben. She is powerless to do anything but go through another night waiting for her husband.

Suddenly, a field hand comes rushing up to the kitchen door. He tells Martha that he's seen both James and Hurricane heading towards the house. Martha rushes upstairs to tell her mistress the news.

"Is Dr. Eben with them?" she asks.

"Dun know, 'mam." answers Martha.

Margaret grabs her shawl and runs towards the front door. The wind has picked up once again and blows the door open violently. She grabs a lantern and walks out onto the porch. She can see the outline of a man, a carriage and three horses. She is thrilled. They have returned. She calls out to Martha to fix a hot plate of food for the men. They will definitely need it after their journey.

The carriage approaches the front of the house. Margaret watches as Hurricane jumps off and stands by the horses. She sees her brother James step out of the carriage, too. She waits for a third figure but it does not come. James slowly walks up to Margaret and takes her by both arms.

"Let us go inside, dear sister." James tells her.

"Where is my husband?" She asks.

James lowers his head and again asks Margaret to go inside.

"Where is Eben?!"

James and Margaret enter the front hallway. James is cold and seems shaken. "We could not find him,sister. We got as far as the ferry and found his horse had been unhitched and roaming freely. We then saw his carriage caught in the mud on the side of the road. But no one was there."

"Maybe he walked to his friend's home...he could still be there."

"Dear sister, we went to town and no one has seen him."

Margaret slowly sits down with a look of disbelief on her face.

"He is there. My husband is at his friend's home. He must be!"

James has little more to add to his story. Margaret continues to sit and shake her head back and forth repeating the same phrase over and over again.

'He is there. He must be!"

Alice can hear the commotion going on in the front hallway. She carefully climbs out of bed and walks towards the stairs. She can tell by the tone of everyone's voices that it is not good news. But, she is curious to see what is happening and listens in. From the staircase, she watches as her mother lowers her head into her hands. Alice begins to creep down the stairs. She gets to the bottom and quietly walks towards her mother. Alice taps on her mother's shoulder. Her mother is unaware her daughter is beside her.

"Mother, are you sick?"

James rushes over and picks Alice up and holds her close. Alice squirms around to get out of his grasp. James holds her tighter and takes her out of the room. He falls to one knee and places Alice on the other.

"Alice, my sweet girl, your mother has much on her mind. You must be good and take ye back to your bed. Martha and Sista will tuck you in."

Martha quickly walks over and picks up Alice. She motions to Sista to come along and they begin ascending the stairs. Martha notices the three boys sitting on the landing. They make a dash for their rooms before she can say anything to them. Martha enters Alice's room and tucks her back in bed.

"Can Sista stay a while?" Alice asks.

"Only fa' a bit." answers Martha.

The two girls curl up on the bed. Alice beneath the sheets and Sista wrapped up in a crocheted blanket by her side. The two girls are inseparable and will need each other's comfort over the next few days.

Margaret lifts up her head and pushes herself up from the chair, almost losing her balance. James goes to catch her but she puts her hand up to stop him. She slowly heads back to her room and sits in her rocking chair. She gazes out her window and repeats over and over to herself, *'He'll be back tomorrow. He will be back tomorrow'.*

Hurricane has decided to take the horses back to the stable. He knows they will not be going out again this night. But, he knows he will be asked again to search for the doctor. He knows what this means if they cannot find him. There may be a lot of changes going on with the plantation. If the doctor is gone, would Margaret be able to stay in charge? Would Reverend Belin take over? He needs to get back to his wife, Martha and his daughter. He is exhausted and is in much discomfort from the freezing cold.

Once done putting the horses up for the night, Hurricane makes his way back to the main house to see if he is needed in the morning. He already knows the answer. He and the Reverend will go out again until his master is found...dead or alive.

He enters through the kitchen door. Martha is making her way down the back staircase. They embrace without saying a word. They hold on to each as if someone or something were trying to tear them apart. Martha looks up at Hurricane, but he only shakes his head side to side. He already knows what she is about to ask. He releases his hold of Martha, turns around and heads to the parlor to talk to Reverend Belin.

The next morning at sunrise, James and Hurricane are again in the carriage. They have decided to visit some of the homes in Georgetown and ask if anyone has seen Dr. Eben. Margaret continues to watch through the window from her rocking chair. She has not moved throughout the night. She blows out the candle that was lit in the window and pulls herself up. The children will be down soon and will ask too many questions. She must wash, change clothes and put on a brave face. She must prepare herself for this day.

Martha goes upstairs to wake the children. The boys are already awake and dressing, but Alice is still asleep. She and Sista were still curled up like two small rabbits. Martha picks up Sista and puts her in a chair. She wakes Alice and gets her ready for the day.

Alice takes one look at Martha and asks, "Father?"

Martha turns away. She clears her throat and says "Nah, he be at a frend house. Time ta go dun stairs."

Alice does as she is told and continues to dress. She smiles at Martha and runs through the door to look for her mother.

The children find Margaret at the dining table. They can see she is worn and her eyes are bloodshot. They are afraid to ask about their father. The atmosphere in the house seems gray and cold. They sit down and prepare to eat. Alice enters and runs to her mother.

"Father?"

Margaret gives a faint smile and tells her baby girl that he has not come back. Before Alice can say another word, Margaret points to Alice's chair. She walks towards it and slowly sits down. Alice looks at her brothers. Allard sits across from her and he can hardly look her in the eyes. She looks at Arthur and Eben. Neither one raises their heads. But even though Alice is only 4 years old, she can feel the tension in the room and starts her morning meal quietly.

Another day has gone by. No word yet regarding Dr. Eben. Margaret sits and waits by her front parlor window. What is left of last night's candle is burning on the window sill. She is dozing off in her chair having not slept the night before.

Something startles her. A sound of boots on the porch steps.

'They are back!" she thinks to herself.

She runs to the door, swings it open and finds her brother and Hurricane on the porch lowering a large dark woolen blanket to the floor. There is something wrapped in it.

Margaret cannot move. She only stares at the woolen blanket and backs away from the doorway. James can not speak. He rushes to Margaret to hold her, but she continues to back up.

"NOOO!" she cries out and falls to her knees.

"NO, NO, NOOO!"

James reaches down to assist Margaret off the floor. She looks over James' shoulder again at the site on her porch steps. She collapses and continues to cry out. The house servants hear the wailing coming from the parlor and rush in. They already know what has happened. They hold on to themselves for comfort. Their master is dead.

Martha pushes past the others and rushes to her mistress. She and James pick Margaret up and take her to a chair. She continues to mumble the word, 'No' over and over again. James instructs Martha to fetch Margaret a glass of sherry. As she takes a drink, she sees her children watching from the upstairs loft.

Margaret lifts her head, stands up and brushes herself off. She calmly pushes her hair away from her face and walks towards the stairs. Her dress scrapes across the wood floor. She slowly begins to ascend the staircase. It feels like an eternity reaching the top. Once on the landing, she glances down at her 4 surviving children. With all the strength she can muster, she takes a deep breath and softly states, "Your father is dead."

She tells herself that she does not have the luxury of losing her emotions. She has children to think of. She has the plantation to run. She has slaves in her care. She must face the inevitable. She must be strong. Death has once more knocked on the family's door and has entered. She will stand vigilant and protect what she has left. No one, not even death, will stand in her way.

The children look at each other with wide eyes and mouths open. Alice does not understand what has happened. The boys rush to their mother's arms. They surround her and hold her tight. Margaret stands erect not wishing to let her tears fall in front of the children. She gently caresses their heads. She notices Alice standing a few feet away. She reaches out to take her hand. Alice runs back to her room and jumps into her bed.

Martha and Sista climb the stairs. Margaret, still surrounded by her sons, points to Alices' room and gestures for Martha and Sista to go in.

Sista runs to Alice but Martha holds her back.

"Why is everyone so sad?" asks Alice.

"My poor liddle chile. Yo daddy gone ta his homecomin'."

Alice still is not sure what has happened. Martha takes her in her arms and cradles her softly.

"He gone ta be wif de Lawd, chile. He be wif de Lawd."

The next few days will be the most difficult the family will face. Mirrors are covered throughout the house. The parlor is dressed in black crepe. A black crepe wreath hangs on the front door. Portraits are placed face down.

Dr Eben's body is being prepared for the three day wake. Friends and neighbors are beginning to hear the news and are coming by carriage to pay their respects. A couple local plantation women, including James' wife Charlotte, are helping Margaret clean and dress the doctor. He will be laid out in a wooden box draped in velvet and crepe in the parlor.

Margaret must also dress the children in their funeral ware. Alice's dress must be made quickly with what is left of the black crepe and cotton fabrics. Alice is confused by the people who are staying at their home night and day. People donate their time to sit with the good doctor morning, noon and night. It is tradition to do so to make sure the person has actually gone to the Lord and to keep away any evil spirits.

Alice can also hear people talking faintly. She can only make out a few words but did not understand their meanings. The words death, apoplexy and cerebral bleed were whispered between the mourners.

When the day of the funeral arrives, a procession of horses and carriages line the road. James offered his land in Cedar Hill to his sister for the burial. She had buried two of her sons there but Margaret decided to take him to All Saints Parish in Pawleys Island instead. He was a physician for the parish and she knew he would rest in peace beneath the oaks.

This would be a day that Margaret will never forget. The day she was to take over as the matriarch of the Belin/Flagg clan. With the help of her brother, James they will manage the plantation together. They must also prepare Allard to take over some day. It had been James' wish for Allard to take over the plantation when he reached adulthood and that time was approaching. At 15, he would soon be ready to return to his studies and eventually train to be a physician, just like his father. All three boys would follow in their father's footsteps.

And as for Alice. This day would hit her very hard. She has been brought into the parlor to say her last goodbye to her father. The procession to the cemetery is to begin. Margaret takes her by the hand and leads her to the wooden box her father has been laid in. Alice holds her ground. She is a little frightened by what she is about to see.

"Alice, you must say your farewell."

But she cannot utter a word. Only a tear. She now understands.

Chapter Five

The days have passed into years at Wachesaw. Margaret has worked diligently to keep the plantation running...and making money. For a woman to be in charge of hundreds of acres and dozens of slaves is nearly unheard of. Gentlemen of the region who know of Margaret's single and financial status have come to call upon her. But, the last thing she is in need of is someone telling her how to manage her affairs. She has become increasingly strong and at the same time, cold. She has learned to swallow her feelings and put her own personal needs aside. The most important thing is that her children become self-sufficient and keep the legacy of the family alive. And, to keep the money and property in the family as well.

Her father-in-law has recently mismanaged his affairs and almost lost the area of Sandy Island that her family owns. She will not make that same mistake. In fact, she has been buying slaves and increasing the labor force so she can continue to increase her standing. She also is spending more time with Alice and showing her that a woman can achieve anything she sets her mind to.

But, Alice is at that age where she thinks more with her heart than with her mind. She has been spending much of the year at her boarding school, Miss Murden's Seminary for Young Ladies in Charleston. This is one of the finest schools for young women. Margaret believes that Alice needs to learn to manage her own affairs and not completely rely on the wisdom of a man. Of course she would like to see Alice married and have children of her own, but it must be to a particular gentleman. Someone who also has many holdings and is financially stable. But, it seems Alice has been neglecting her studies recently. At 14, she seems only interested in one thing...love.

While in Charleston she has met a number of families of wealth and power. Each family has introduced a son or cousin to the petite, auburn-haired Alice. But, she does not seem too interested in these gents. Conversations always turn to money, status in the community or other selfish pursuits. Alice becomes bored quickly as they boast and brag of their holdings...actually future holdings. It is their fathers that still hold the purse strings. Alice finds it presumptuous of them to believe that they are already the masters of the plantations. They are beginning to sound like her brother, Allard.

Allard was always looked upon as the one who would achieve anything he put his heart into. He was the only one helping his mother with the business decisions in regard to Wachesaw. It is Reverend Belin's wish that it would go to him when he reached adulthood. Margaret, who was to give the plantation to Allard upon his 21st birthday, is still very much in charge. He spent his days in Charleston studying medicine and his time on the plantation was rare. Once out of medical school he came back to Wachesaw and saw his mother's grip still tight on the family bank account. So now that he has achieved his diploma, he must now prepare for his future. He was to marry the daughter of the richest man in Georgetown County, South Carolina. Actually, the entire state. Penelope Ward was his fiance' and the daughter of Joshua John Ward. Joshua John Ward owned 6 plantations from Murrells Inlet to Charleston and his net worth was $500,000. Once Allard is married, he and his bride will live at the new home being built on the inlet...along with Margaret. Margaret had already given it a name...The Hermitage. It is due to her ability to keep the plantation running that the home is being built. The home by the marsh is breathtaking and is located next to Reverend Belin's home. The reverend is also quite impressed with the home and is helping in any way he can in the construction.

When Alice visits the inlet, she rushes to the house to see the progress. The slaves are being quite meticulous with the engravings and architectural designs. Many were sent to work with other carpenters in the area and have become quite skilled in construction. Margaret is pleased with the work but is trying to rush them to complete the build before Allard marries. He has chosen well and accomplished much. All her children have done well. Allard and Eben Jr are both physicians while Arthur is still in medical school. She now has one more to go. She herself has chosen a man for Alice and is looking forward to bringing the two together. He is one of the Alstons.

The Alstons have lived and prospered in the Waccamaw Neck region for decades. They were some of the first to settle the area and create their wealth from rice production. Both families are quite successful and it was always mentioned that it would be a good match bringing the Alstons and the Flaggs together by marriage.

But Alice was not interested in her mother's choice for a husband or any of the young men she had met. She could not see herself married to any of the young men she had been introduced to. She would become quite bored listening to them drone on and on regarding their wealth. They never once asked her what her interests were. What her desires are. Her dreams. And she was not interested in living in a mansion in Charleston. She wanted to stay on the marsh in Murrells Inlet.

The Hermitage was her dream home. She would own it one day. She would dream of sitting by the inlet with her brood of children and reading stories to them. Her heart would be full of love for her husband. He would be a successful man but on his own merit. He would take an interest in her and what she had to say. He would love the inlet as much as she. Her imagination would run wild about her future husband even while she was at school. Her teacher was constantly complaining to her mother how young Alice was spending too much time daydreaming instead of on her studies.

Alice knew whom she would marry. She had met him briefly while she was visiting friends in Georgetown. Her friends lived only blocks away from the harbor and much was going on there. Storekeepers and vendors were out in force peddling their goods. Ships were being loaded with cargo like cotton, rice and pine tar pitch used in ship building. Turpentine would be created from the pine tar and was a much needed material at the naval stores, not only for ship building, but for lamps, liniments and insecticides.

Alice was just leaving one of these stores along the harbor when a very tall, young man in a mad dash to get through the door accidentally stepped on the trane of her dress. Alice momentarily loses her balance and falls back into the arms of the gentleman. Alice is quite embarrassed and alarmed by her situation. For this to happen in public was cause for talk. She quickly adjusts herself and turns towards the young man.

"I am so terribly sorry. Please, my humblest apologies...Miss?"

Alice is dumbfounded and speechless. She was ready to chastise the man, but stopped when she looked into his blue eyes. All she can do is clear her throat.

"Oh no, I am afraid I have caused damage to your dress"

Alice finally looks away from his blue eyes and notices the hem of her gown has been torn.

"Oh, this will not do." Alice responds.

"Please, I beg, do not think me forward, but if I may have your name and where you reside, I can pay to have your dress repaired."

Alice is still a bit stunned. Her friends are waving to her to come back to their residence and she knows she can not stay much longer.

"I am Miss Flagg... Miss Alice Flagg. But I am only a visitor to Georgetown. I must return to Miss Murden's School in Charleston in 2 days time."

"Then I will call upon you to right this wrong. Again, my humblest apologies."

The young man bows quickly and turns to leave, still in quite the hurry.

"What be your name, sir?" Alice cries out, then suddenly realizes she has raised her voice in public and is receiving harsh looks from the crowd of onlookers.

He turns around and with a slight grin replies,"Brannock...Johnathan Risley Brannock."

Alice watches as the young man runs towards the docks heading for one of the ships. She feels a pulling on her sleeve and realizes it is her friends. They smile and giggle at Alice and take her by the arm.

As they walk back to the house, Alice can only think about this blue-eyed gent. This is the one time she is actually looking forward to going back to school in Charleston. She hopes he hasn't forgotten her name or the school where she attends.

Alice and her friends walk several blocks back to the house she is staying in. On this trip her mother was under the weather and could not accompany Alice back to school so she allows Sista to go with her this time. Sista is the only person Alice can truly talk to. Alice could tell anything to Sista and know she will take it to her grave.

Alice enters the home and heads straight upstairs. Sista is waiting just outside her bedroom door.

"Where ya be?" asks Sista. "Ya be late fer supper."

"Oh, Sista! My mind is a whirl and my heart beats so."

Sista notices a blush on Alices' cheeks.

"What y'all be up ta?"

"Sista, I have just met my future husband."

Sista bends her head sideways and puts her hands on her hips.

"Oh Lawd...who'dit be? One o' tem Astons?"

Alice starts to answer, but stops mid sentence. She clears her throat over and over and sits on the bed. Her breathing becomes raspy. She stares at Sista and points towards the bedroom bureau. She is now gasping and wheezing. Sista knows what to do. She pulls open the drawer and finds a small greenish colored bottle. She hands it to Alice and she begins to drink from it. It is a special cocktail her mother and brother Allard had created for her. Her breathing is still labored and she lies down upon the bed. Sista begins to prop pillows behind her head.

"Slow 'n deep...slow 'n deep," sista repeats over and over.

Alice slowly takes in deep breaths listening to Sista's coaching. She holds Sista's hand and begins to calm down. Her breathing is less labored.

Alice is afflicted with what the family calls 'spells'. She and Allard both have mild afflictions with asthma especially in damp climates. Allard would smoke a mix of stramonium and tobacco to soothe his spasms but a young woman would take the stramonium powder and place it in hot water to inhale. But here in Georgetown, she only had her mix of coffee and opium to calm her. Sista would spend the night watching over Alice, making sure she did not take too much of the medicine.

While Alice rests, Sista notices the hem of her dress. She sits quietly on the edge of the bed with needle and thread and mends the fabric. She knows Alice will be resting for quite a while and dinner will have to wait. She will sleep quietly through this night.

It is time for Alice to travel to Charleston once again for school. It will take a good part of the day to arrive and she is still quite tired from the day before. The carriage rocks her back and forth. She begins to drift off to sleep with Sista beside her. Before she knows it, they are in Charleston.

Charleston is quite a big city to Alice. Almost overwhelming. The noise and constant clatter of hooves on the streets: people chattering away as they walk along the alleys is annoying to her. The gardens will be blooming again in a month or so with the smell of confederate jasmine heavy in the air. There are two things Alice does like about the city, the gardens and being close to the ocean. The mansions line the streets with immaculate gardens running alongside. Azalea bushes with crimson red and soft white flowers are a must in each landscape. But, the noise keeps Alice from enjoying her time here. Sometimes, she feels she is drowning in the hustle and bustle. She feels as though she doesn't exist. Many of her schoolmates are from the most prominent families and also are confronted with the same dilemma as she. They must marry for money first, profit second and maybe, in a few years love may follow.

Alice can still hear her mother's voice in her head. Whenever she and her mother would discuss Alice's future betrothed, her mother would tell her to '*marry for status*' or ' *eventually you will learn to love him*'. And the one her mother constantly repeats... '*Love does not put food on thy table.*'

There was one time years ago when Alice noticed her mother gazing at her father's framed portrait. It had been nearly a year after her father passed and it was a difficult subject to bring up. Her mother did not speak much of her father unless it was in regard to a debt that was owed or how the finances were not where they ought to be due his procrastination balancing his ledgers.

But one day, Alice drew the courage to speak and ask her mother if she was in love with her husband when they married.

Margaret turned the portrait over and placed it face down in a drawer, slowly closed it and answered, "I was content."

Alice was not 'content' with her mother's answer and pressed on.

Margaret turned and looked at Alice. Alice knew that particular look meant they were done talking. It was all Margaret would say on the subject. But Alice thought she saw a tender moment in her mother's eyes when she gazed at her father's portrait. And it may be another year before her mother would look upon her husband's face again.

So all Alice knows of love is how she feels about her blue-eyed stranger. She is anxious to see him again and hopes he feels the same.

Days have passed and there is still no sign of her blue-eyed Johnathan. She constantly looks out windows in search of him. It won't be an easy task to receive him at an all girl's boarding school. The rules are strict when it comes to visitors. Especially if it concerns a young man making a call on one of the girls. Miss Murden is quite adamant that a young lady should have a chaperone when with a young suitor. There are particular hours and days the visitor may make a house call and all this must go through Miss Murden.

This concerns Alice. Miss Murden knows Alice's mother has made it quite clear that Alice is to someday marry one of the Alstons. So, to go about this will take some imagination on Alice's part. She will have to rely on Sista to be her go-between, her messenger and ally. She and Sista will have to work out a plan so Alice may see her suitor without the interference of Miss Murden.

Then, one afternoon when Alice and some other schoolgirls are in the music room, a knock comes to the door. One of the house servants answers and there is a tall, young man standing at the door. Alice can not hear what is being said but turns to look into the hallway. The servant allows the gentleman into the hall and takes his hat. She asks him to stay while she fetches the mistress of the school. As soon as she leaves, Alice runs from the music room into the hall.

"Ah, Miss Flagg, correct?"

"Yes, Mr Brannock. It is good of you to come."

He holds out his hand and takes hers. He raises it up and offers a light kiss. Alice feels her cheeks flush and gives a slight curtsy.

"I am so sorry for my delay, however I had to complete the business at hand in Georgetown before making my way to Charleston. Will you forgive me?"

"Mr Brannock, I accept your apology, again."

"Ah, yes...your dress. How may I right this terrible wrong?"

"It has been corrected, Mr Brannock."

But before Johnathan can start his sentence, Miss Murden walks into the room. Sista has followed her down the steps and sees the young man with Alice.

Miss Murden shakes her head and faces Alice. "To the music room, Miss Flagg."

Alice turns to say her good-bye to Johnathan but she is blocked by Miss Murden. "To the music room, now"

Alice gazes once more into Johnathon's eyes, curtsies and walks away. Miss Murden closes the pocket doors to the room and turns towards Johnathan.

" I do not allow my girls to receive visitors nor suitors without my permission or knowledge. May I ask who you are and your business here?"

"I am Johnathan Brannock. I only came to see Miss Flagg. We had an unfortunate accident recently and I am here to inquire if she is in need of further assistance."

"Well, Miss Flagg has not conveyed to me that she is in need of any assistance. If so, I will offer it to her. Good day, sir."

"Good day, mam." Johnathan turns towards the door and sees it is already open by the houseservant. He takes his hat from the servant, bows and leaves.

Miss Murden opens the doors to the music room and asks the other girls to give her and Alice a private moment. The girls leave, giggling to themselves while Miss Murden walks over to Alice.

"Miss Flagg, I believe after your extensive time here at the school you are aware of the house rules, are you not?"

"Yes, Miss Murden."

"Then, you are aware that you are not to invite gentlemen to this establishment without my consent."

"I did not invite him. He mirely came to ask if he could..."

Miss Murden interrupts Alice. "Miss Flagg, I am not going to entertain this dialogue anymore. Please go to your room. This will not take place again. Understand?"

"Yes, mam." Alice answers. She turns and ascends the stairs, stomping her feet on each step. She knows Miss Murden is watching and as she enters her room, slams her door shut. Sista slowly enters the room. She's not certain if this is a good decision or not. She sees Alice is face down in her bed crying into her pillow. Sista runs over to comfort Alice.

"Dun' be sad, Miss. Ya make ya'self sick."

"Oh Sista, did you see him? That is my Johnathan that I told you of."

Alice dries off her tears and turns over in bed facing Sista. She knows she must hatch a plan to see her love again. But, how?

The following day is a beautiful one. It is Sunday and the weather in Charleston is becoming warmer each day. The girls of the school are walking towards church. Miss Murden is in the front of the procession of girls. Alice is walking slowly today and is last in line. She is depressed that she may not see her beau.

The congregation enters the church and the girls take their places in the pews. Before Alice takes her seat, she feels a tap on her shoulder. She lifts her head and sees Johnathan. He smiles and takes a seat behind her. She blushes and smiles coyly. She cannot concentrate on the minister's words but continues to look over her shoulder throughout the mass. When it is time to sing the homily, she can hear Johnathan's voice. It is strong and carries throughout the church. She bites her lip. She's afraid everyone will turn to look at him and see the expression on her face. She can't give away her feelings. She must keep this a secret. Especially from Miss Murden. She has probably already written to her mother about the events of the previous day. She must let Johnathan know that this cannot be an open relationship. But, will he leave her if she tells him this? Will he feel it is not worth the aggravation of pursuing a girl whose family has other plans for her future? She will have to find out.

Once mass is over, the girls line up like ducklings behind Miss Murden and follow her out of the building. Alice stays to the back of the line watching for Johnathan. She sees him waiting behind an oak tree along the sidewalk. As Miss Murden passes by, he keeps watch that she does not notice him. The minute Alice walks by, he reaches out and takes her by the hand, pulling her towards the tree. She is a little surprised by his advance. But, she is full of excitement. The two stand facing each other holding hands, still trying to hide behind the tree.

"I apologize for taking hold of you this way, but I wanted to see you."

"It seems each time we meet, Mr Brannock, you are apologizing to me for your aggressive approach." Alice laughs and so does Johnathan.

"It seems Miss Flagg, that you cause me to be unsure of myself and stumble at my approach. I came to tell you I will be in Charleston longer than expected and I do hope you will give me the honor of calling on you again."

"Miss Murden has made it impossible for me to have guests. She and my mother have other plans for my future, which I do not wish to be a party of. If we are to meet, it may be only in private, I am afraid."

"Oh, so it is to be a mission or should I say ...a challenge that I may persuade your teacher and family to allow us to meet."

"Mr Brannock, it will be quite the challenge when it comes to my family. But, for now, I must end our visit before I am chastised by Miss Murden. But, but...I do hope to have the pleasure of seeing you again soon."

"Please...call me Johnathan. I look forward to our next rondevu."

Johnathan takes her hand and places a note inside. Alice puts the note inside her glove and rushes off.

She runs as fast as she can to Miss Murden's. She sees the last of the girls entering the building. Miss Murden steps out the door and sees Alice running towards her. Alice suddenly stops and bows her head. She is ready for another bout with her mistress.

"Miss Flagg, why do you linger so? Get inside and ready for supper."

"Yes, mam."Alice answers, beads of sweat on her brow. She swiftly runs through the entryway and returns to her room. She jumps on her bed and begins to read Johnathan's note. Sista has finished cleaning the room and glances over at Alice. She is slowly smiling and quickly hides the note.

"Miz Alice...ya' be a'right?"

"More than just all right, Sista. I am the happiest I have ever been!"

Alice takes Sista by the hand and sits her down on her bed. She has thought of a way she can still see Johnathan. But, it will take the help of her best friend Sista to accomplish her plan.

Over the following weeks, Alice and Johnathan have been exchanging notes. The first letter Johnathan had sent her mentioned where he would be staying in Charleston. It would be impossible for Alice to leave school and see him, so she sent Sista to deliver a letter to Johnathan. Alice knew there was a cemetery next door to Johnathan's residence. Alice requested Johnathan to leave their love letters in a space between the bricks to the entrance of the graveyard. Sista would return to Alice with a new letter every day and Alice would hand her another in response to his. This would carry on for several weeks. With each letter they would exchange information about their hopes and dreams. On one particular day Alice received another letter, the envelope was marked urgent. Johnathan was getting ready to leave Charleston and head back to Georgetown. He and his father had business to conclude and he did not know how long he would be gone. He must see her before they leave.

Jonathan had told Alice all about his life and business affairs through the letters. He and his father owned many hundreds of acres in North Carolina and were coming to South Carolina to buy more property. The property would not be used to grow cotton or rice but to produce turpentine.

Naval stores were rising up all along the North and South Carolina coasts and pine tar was very important in the ship building business. His father would be acquiring land in Horry and Georgetown Counties that grew the highest number of longleaf pine trees. Not only was turpentine used in ship building industries, but it was needed in disinfectants, medical soaps and printing inks. It was incredibly demanding work and many slaves were used in tapping the trees. Johnathan had to travel from North to South Carolina often, but was hoping to stay in Georgetown County and run the business from there.

Alice was saddened to hear he was leaving again, but then she noticed a postscript at the bottom of his letter.

'When I return, dearest Alice, I believe it will be the proper time for an introduction to your brother and mother. Dearest regards, your Johnathan.'

Alice held her breath as she read the note. Meeting her family before she finished school would not be well received. Not to mention her mother's plans for her future. She had told him previously she would be in Charleston until May and then travel to Murrells Inlet. There she will meet with her mother before leaving for the mountains to escape the summer heat. Alice would have to muster the courage to have her family meet Johnathan and hope he could persuade them to accept their union.

Alice quickly scribbled another note and handed it to Sista. She knew she must see him before he leaves town. She hoped to convince Miss Murden that she was going for a walk after the evening meal with Sista. Then, she will sneak away to rendezvous with Johanthan.

'This has to work...it must.' Alice thought to herself.

Sista scurried down the stairs towards the back door. She quickly wrapped her shawl around her shoulders and as she grabbed the door handle another hand appeared. It was Miss Murden's.

"And where are you going in such haste?"

Sista knows it doesn't look good for a slave to be running out a door. She had only seconds to come up with a believable answer.

"I...I...I bees sick 'n dun wanna mess ya' pritty carpit."

Miss Murden backed away. "Go on then, quickly."

Sista rushed through the door and leaned over some azalea bushes pretending to lose her supper.

"Heaven's NO, not there. Over there!" Miss Murden cried out.

This gave Sista the opportunity to run to the side of the house out of Miss Murden's sight. She quietly snuck through the back garden gate and to the cemetery.

The night was falling and it began to get misty outside. Alice was quite nervous about the change in weather. How could she convince Miss Murden she wanted to go for a good night stroll in the rain? Miss Murden would catch on immediately. The only way to escape would be to sneak away after lights out. She would be late meeting Johnathan and prayed he would still be there waiting for her.

Dinner seemed like an eternity and Alice was hoping to be dismissed from the table soon. The other girl's had other things on their minds and did not seem to pay attention to Alices' eagerness to leave.

Finally, dinner was cleared away and Alice made her way back to her room. She would have to quietly make her way downstairs later that evening to see Johnathan. The wind had started to pick up and became gusty. It was not going to be easy venturing out in this weather.

Sista takes Alice aside and tells her about the close call she had with Miss Murden earlier. She looked out the window and saw the weather become worse.

"Miz Alice, y'all shoodn't go out 'n dis."

"I have to Sista, I just must."

Alice covers herself with her cape and quietly creeps out the back door. Sista kept Miss Murden's servants busy in the slave quarters so Alice could make her way without being seen. The damp air was not making her journey easy but she made it to the cemetery. She looked all around the area, up and down the alleys but there was no sign of Johnathan. She had missed him by only minutes. Jonathan could stay no longer and went back to his residence.

Alice knew she must get back to Miss Murden's soon, but continued to wait by the wrought iron gate. The gate swung to and fro with a terrible creaking noise. After what felt like hours, Alice made her way back to Miss Murden's. Once she got to her room, she collapsed on her bed. Her breathing had become labored. She was having another 'spell'. Sista was in her quarters and Alice had to search for her medicine. After a few tense moments she found it. She was having a difficult time swallowing. She wanted to cry out, but the words stuck in her throat. She had not changed out of her wet clothes and knew if she went to Miss Murden she would ask too many questions. But she was beginning to become light-headed and had trouble focusing. She made it to her bedroom door and fainted.

Chapter Six

"Alice...Alice, wake up."

Alice hears a familiar voice. "Brother?" she answers.

She slowly opens her eyes and sees her brother Arthur by her bed placing a cold cloth upon her brow. Alice is beginning to catch her breath, her breathing has become easier.

"Little sister, you have given the household a fright! Are you feeling comfortable now?"

Alice nods her head. She imagines all her schoolmates must know her secret by now. She has always been quite shy in regards to her asthma. If this secret is out, maybe her private affair with Johnathan is out in the open as well.

"Alice, Miss Murden called upon me at my school. You seem to be in better spirits currently so I will sit with you only a short while longer. Can you answer this? Had you gone out in this foul weather? I only ask due to the condition of your dress when I arrived. You know this is not conducive to your condition."

Alice whispers to her brother, "Please brother, let us not speak of this. I will explain the circumstances another time."

Arthur softly smiles at Alice and agrees to discuss the matter later. He leaves the room to report to Alice's teacher. Alice takes a very deep breath and lets out a small whimper. She is trying desperately to hold back the tears. She has missed her chance to see Johnathan and does not know when the opportunity will present itself.

After speaking with the head mistress, Arthur quietly knocks on Alice's door and enters. Many of the students would be leaving for school break the following week and he and Miss Murden have decided to let Alice go back home a few days early to recoup. Arthur has agreed to escort his sister back to Murrells Inlet. He advises Sista to pack her things and they will leave for home in the morning.

Arthur and Alice's trip was a pleasant one. Alice made sure to keep her brother occupied on other subjects so he would not ask about her predicament the day before. She kept his mind on his own medical studies, constantly asking him about the latest breakthroughs in medicine and how he liked his professors. Before they knew it, they were in Georgetown. Arthur did not want to exhaust Alice, so they were to stay the night by the harbor.

Alice looked out upon the harbor watching the sloops sailing in and all she could think of was her Johnathan. She now had another worry on her mind. Here she is ...a girl of only 14 years and 5 months who believes she loves a man of 17. Her youth does not seem to bother Johnathan. Alice's family has introduced her to gentlemen nearly 10 years her senior and hope once she was done with her formal education she would marry right away. But she knows her family will not approve of Johnathan due to his status. How will she explain this to her family? His family business is a profitable one and he does have a future. But, Johnathan travels to different locations to manage his father's business and would be gone often. Not only that, she knows there are times he himself has helped out physically with the tapping of the trees for pitch. How would they perceive him? As a man of business or common laborer?

Alice and her brother spend the night and are up all the earlier the next day to finish their trip to Murrells Inlet. She does look forward to seeing the inlet and is excited about the construction on the Hermitage. She asks Arthur if the home is ready to be lived in and if it would be possible for her to stay there overnight instead of the main house by the river.

" I do not know if it is wise to stay while construction still carries on. Remember your situation. It will be up to Allard and mother to decide."

Alice shrugs her shoulders. When she is ill she usually gets her way. The last thing the family wants to do is upset her while she is recuperating.

The carriage makes its way towards the main house. Alice again asks her brother if they may go to the Hermitage instead. She gives a long pout and grabs hold of his hand.

"Mother is expecting us at the main house. We shall go there and you may demonstrate your case to her."

As the carriage draws near the house, Margaret is seen on the front porch. She has a smile on her face and her arms are outstretched to receive them both. Arthur opens the carriage door and assists Alice down the steps. She is cautious when approaching her mother. She does not know if news regarding her conduct at school has reached her mother's ears. Margaret reaches out and holds Alice tightly, but only for a moment. She goes from joy to concern in a matter of seconds.

"My child, my poor child. Quickly, let us get you upstairs and put you to bed."

"Mother, please...may I go to the Hermitage to regain my strength? The heat of the day is approaching and I would breathe easier if by the inlet."

"Daughter, I have everything prepared here. You will rest here and perhaps before we leave for the north, we will make a stop at Hermitage to inspect our future home."

Alice bowed her head and headed up the staircase. Sista turned toward Margaret and asked to be excused to see her mother, Martha. Margaret agreed that after she unpacked Alice's things she could see Martha.

Sista ran hastily up the stairs with one of Alice's bags. She found Alice sitting at her writing desk staring into her mirror. She would do this often when she was in deep thought. Always daydreaming, always conjuring up a future for herself in the mirror.

"Miz Alice, awright if I goes sees my momma?"

Alice doesn't pay attention to Sista. She only continues to stare into the mirror hoping and wishing. Sista asks again and Alice nods. Sista runs out of her room and down the back staircase towards the kitchen. There she finds Martha preparing supper for the Flaggs.

Martha spins around and grabs hold of her daughter nearly lifting her off the ground. They hold each other tight for what seems like hours. Suddenly, Martha realizes she has to pay attention to what she's doing. She almost burned the mid day meal.

"Lawdy, chile, I is so glad ya' home."exclaims Martha.

"Where paw at?"

The expression on Martha's face changes suddenly. Taking a deep breath, she pauses and tells Sista of the current events.

"Ya pa' been hurted, Sista. He dun gots hurt by the tack horse. He ain't too bad, but it be a while b'fore he can work."

"Kin I sees 'um?"

Martha smiles and tells her that Hurricane is back at the driver's shack. Sista rushes out the door and heads towards the slave quarters. She reaches the location and stops by the door. She quietly knocks before entering. She hears her father's voice answer. She walks through and finds Dr. Allard there bandaging Hurricane's hand. He sits up and grins at his daughter.

Dr. Allard reaches into his medical bag and walks towards the door.

"Do not fret, Sista. Your father is stronger than any horse. He will heal eventually. I will give you instructions for his care."

Sista runs to him and he holds her with his right arm. Hurricane is embarrassed to show his left hand. It had been crippled by one of the mares. She slowly takes hold of his injured hand and draws it towards her. A tear flows down Sista's face. Hurricane takes her back into his arms and holds her tight.

"There now, chile, I bees jus' fine."

Dr. Allard hands Sista some cotton cloth and disinfectant. He explains that she or Martha must keep the wound clean. His hand would be swollen and bruised, but did not see anything broken. Sista bows her head to Dr. Allard and curls up with her father on his bed.

"I believe it is time for me to return to my family. Let us hope I am done with my rounds today and will have a quiet night with them."

Dr. Allard leaves their shack and mounts his horse. He takes a moment to reflect on the conditions of the homes in the slave quarters. Allard has had many visits here lately for medical reasons. There seems to be an increase in accidents but something else has occurred. The infant mortality rate has been increasing. In a small, makeshift graveyard, he sees small markers of the children who did not survive. As a physician, he can only do so much. Malaria, tuberculosis, and especially yellow fever have been rearing their ugly heads throughout the region. His brother, Eben Jr. has decided to take residence in Charleston and continue his practice there. Allard must stay. It is up to him and his brother Arthur, who will be out of medical school soon to care for the slaves and their own family.

Allard notices the time and rides swiftly back home. He is looking forward to seeing his little sister Alice. He is hoping her studies have gone well. Margaret and he have found the perfect suitor for her. They are hoping to have a gathering before leaving for the north.

As Allard rides up the alley towards his home, he sees a stranger on horseback coming along the trail. He stops and watches a young man approach him. He does not recognize him and stays atop his horse.

"Good day to you, sir. I am hoping to be addressing Dr. Flagg?"

"Good day to you...yes, I am Dr. Allard Flagg. How may I assist you?"

"I apologize for coming unannounced but I am hoping to make yours and your mother's acquaintance. Let me introduce myself. My name is Brannock, Jonathan Brannock. I had the good fortune of meeting your sister, Alice...I mean, Miss Flagg and I hope to find she and your family well."

Dr. Allard is a little unnerved by this unknown gentleman who may be calling on his sister. He will have to meet with Alice and find the story behind this stranger and what his intentions are for her. He needs to learn more about this situation and decides to invite Johnathan to the house.

"Well then, Mr. Brannock. Please, join us at my home. I have only just gotten back from my rounds and have not had the pleasure of welcoming my sister back from Charleston. Follow me."

Both men steer their horses towards the river side home. Once at the front door, both men dismount and walk up towards the door. Dr. Allard asks Johnathan to give him a moment so he may greet his sister alone. He will have a servant prepare something for him to drink. Jonathan waits on the porch while Allard walks in. He immediately instructs one of the servants to take Johnathan to the parlor, bring him a drink and to ask that he stay there.

The servant does just this and Allard rushes upstairs to search out his sister and mother. Both are in Margaret's drawing room discussing Alice's school activities and some of the teacher's remarks from a previous letter Margaret received.

"My little sister is home again. Oh, how we missed your sweet voice in these halls." Allard sweeps Alice up in his arms and places her down gently.

"Dearest brother, oh, how I have missed you and mother! And,of course, home. Charleston seems like a world away. Now, I may find peace among our beautiful foliage and listen to the locusts hum in the night and sing me to sleep."

"We are so glad to see you, child. And, there may be someone else who you will be happy to see as well."

Alice puts on an inquisitive face and tilts her head.

"I believe you have a visitor currently in the downstairs parlor who did not wish you to leave Charleston."

At first, she was puzzled. But then, her eyes widened.

'No, it can't be?!' she thinks to herself.

Margaret also has a puzzled look on her face and asks Allard for an answer to this riddle.

"Let us all go down stairs and meet this gentleman, shall we?" Allard opens the door for both the ladies and Alice hurries as fast as she can down the staircase. She throws open the parlor doors and finds Johnathan sitting by the window. He immediately jumps out of his seat and approaches Alice. They meet halfway and hold hands.

"Johnathan...I thought you had business and had to leave Charleston?"

"I did, but I could not believe you would not have said goodbye to me before my departure? I went back to Miss Murden's but you had left"

But, before Alice can answer his question, she releases his grip and takes a step back. She can hear her mother and brother directly behind her. It is time to introduce Johnathan.

Alice turns to face her family. Dr. Allard takes his mother by the arm and introduces Margaret to Johnathan. Margaret still does not understand the reason for this stranger to be calling on her daughter.

Margaret starts the interview first by asking, "Mr. Brannock, please be seated. May I inquire about the reason behind this visit?"

Johnathan bows to Margaret and takes a seat. Dr. Allard remains standing by the piano. Johnathan and Alice can tell by his stance that he is quite uncomfortable.

Johnathan begins to tell the family about his unusual encounter with Alice in Charleston. Neither Margaret nor Allard seem amused by the story. Alice continues to stare at Johnathan, trying not to look at her family.

Allard interrupts Johnathan and asks, "And, where do your family hail from, Mr Brannock. Are they rice planters as well? I ask because I do not recognize your name."

" No sir, my family has property in North Carolina. We are acquiring more land here in the counties of Georgetown and Horry."

"And, if your family are not planters, then may I ask how you create your income from your land?"

"Pine tar pitch. We produce turpentine and other elements from the tar. We own quite a number of acres of pine barrens. My father has a small dwelling in Georgetown near the harbor where we conduct some of our affairs. The rest of our holdings are in Horry County and south of Charleston. We are hoping to make our way to Georgia in the coming years."

Dr. Allard is not happy with Johnathan's answer. He has always believed the men who are buying the longleaf pines are destroying the trees. He understands there is money to be made from this endeavor but knows that this is the work of a commoner, and considers the people involved in the industry as locusts flying from one tree to the other and then leaving the dead behind. This is absolutely not the type of man who should be involved with his sister. He believes he must end this interview for today.

Margaret is also not excited about this turn of events. She turns towards Allard and watches as he walks towards Johnathan.

"Mr. Brannock, Mrs. Flagg and I wish to take time to discuss this situation. We have been taken off guard and need to discuss this in more detail. So, please do not find me rude, but I must ask you to leave."

Alice is devastated. She knows what Allard means by this. She can tell by his demeanor that he does not wish to discuss this further and has made up his mind in regard to Johnathan.

Alice turns towards Johnathan. He bows to her and walks towards the front door. Allard follows and opens the door for him. Johnathan turns and makes one more attempt to persuade him.

But, the only response he receives is *"Good day, sir"* from Allard.

Johnathan bows his head one more time and walks down the steps towards his horse. Alice runs to the parlor window and watches as her love gallops away down the alley lined with oak trees.

Alice turns to Allard, "Brother, you did not give him a chance. Why would you not see with your own eyes that he is a man of honor and worthy of my love."

Margaret is still seated in her chair. She will let Allard handle the situation as man of the house. But, she herself will talk to Alice alone later once she has learned more about the situation.

"Love? What do you know of the word? We are looking out for your best interest. Your family loves you and knows what is best."

Alice turns to her brother. "Allard, were you not in love when you decided to marry Miss Penelope Ward? No one questioned your honor at receiving her hand, but I am to be married off to a complete stranger only for their standing and status. Why can I not also find love?"

Allard is shocked by her question. "Young lady, do not ask of me what my heart feels or the reason behind my marriage. It is a decision both households were agreeable with. We are only thinking of you, dear child. Do you not understand the life this gentleman offers? Have you not understood that he wanders the countryside? He has no stable home. You wish to stay in your beautiful inlet surrounded by your loving family, do you not? He will take you from here. You must go where he goes. They are like gypsies and your life is here, not to be the bride of a common lumberjack."

Alice is furious with Allard's answer, but takes a moment to think before she speaks again. She feels there is no way around their decision. Atleast, not yet. She will go to the one person she believes will help her. Her Uncle James.

Alice runs from the parlor and up the stairs to her room. She must talk with her Uncle. He may have a more understanding heart. She knows how much he loved his first wife and the pain he felt when he lost her to fever. He would understand and may give a better argument on her behalf. At least, she hopes so.

Later that afternoon, Alice receives a knock on her door. Margaret walks in ...alone. She sits down next to Alice and asks a very important question.

"Alice, dear. I must ask a very serious question. How did you keep in touch with this young man? I specifically know that Miss Murden would not approve of any visitations of this nature. You seem to have much information regarding this man and you seem very adamant to continue this...this 'relationship'. So, I ask of you, how do you know of him and his business beyond the initial meeting? You must have spoken on more than one occasion?"

Alice did not know how to answer her question. This would mean a harsh penalty for her and would end what little chance there was for a relationship between her and Johnathan. Not to mention, Sista. Sista would be in terrible trouble for delivering her letters behind the school mistress's back. She could not bear to see her punished or even worse...sent away. Alice had put herself and Sista in a terrible predicament. She must choose her words carefully.

"It is rather a silly ploy, but I engaged a friend at school to deliver a couple of letters to him. Please, do not ask their name 'fore I will not divulge that information."

Margaret did not completely believe her daughter's story, but did think it possible. She had been young herself once and understands the power of first love. Yes, even she had memories of herself at Alice's age. Dreams sweep away any form of common sense. Margaret could not bear losing her baby girl to such a harsh life. She must continue to watch over her child and keep her from the pain of love. She thought it foolhardy to leave yourself open to someone who would only break your heart. She did not like Mr. Brannock's profession at all. He was a wanderer. And so could be his heart. A man who travels often could open his arms to another. She could not bear that for her daughter. She knew it all too well. She herself had gone through heartache, but did not want her children to know. She had to remain strong for everyone. Alice must marry a man who would bring status, money and control his business in the local area. This way Margaret could also keep watch on Alice's husband so that his eyes may not wander. She did not want her marrying someone who leaves for days or weeks on end without a word, leaving her stranded with children and worry. If Alice were to marry Mr. Brannock, he would take Alice with him to another county or state. And, Margaret may never see her daughter again.

Alice's health was also at stake. She was so frail and needed to be with her and the family. Arthur had talked to her about Alice's latest 'spell' and this concerned her greatly. Her attacks were becoming more frequent and she thought Alice probably did not engage Johnathan in any conversation regarding her health.

But, that wasn't all. Margaret was in control of the accounts and she was not about to allow an outsider to take what she had worked so hard for. All the money brought from the sale of rice, cotton and corn were due to her hard work. And, heartbreak. When her husband would leave for days, it was Margaret who ran everything, but still under his watchful eye. When he passed, it brought both sorrow and relief to her. A love-hate dynamic between the two. She loved him, but also could not release the pain he caused her. She knew he was not completely faithful, but could not prove it. Was it jealous love that made her feel this way? Her thoughts of love had changed over the years. To marry for love brings nothing but heartache but to marry for security seems more important. If Alice were to marry another wealthy planter in Murrells Inlet, Margaret would not worry about losing her money. And, she could still control her daughter. She hoped by doing this, Alice's heart would never break the way her's had.

Margaret holds Alices' hand and brushes her hair away from her face. She begins to walk away towards the door, but stops and relays one more thought. "Then I assume you have discussed your health with Mr.

Brannock and he does not see it as a hindrance? Why, most men would be rather concerned if their future bride were in some way unable to assist with the running of the household as well as other matters."

Alice could not answer right away. That was the one thing she feared. That Johnathan would look upon her sickness as an interference with both his business and household life. She could not let him know.

"I only know that I love him. And he loves me." was Alice's answer.

"So", Margaret asks, "he has told you this himself?"

Alice does not answer and looks away from her mother's gaze.

Margaret walks away and closes the door. She believes she has made her message clear to Alice.

Margaret walks down the staircase and into the parlor where Allard waits. She has a way of taking care of the young Mr. Brannock before the situation becomes more serious. She confides in Allard that she is quite sure Alice has not disclosed her health to Mr. Brannock and that he should be made aware of the situation. If this does not persuade him to stop all contact with Alice, then maybe the announcement of a coming engagement will keep him at bay.

Chapter Seven

Dr. Allard has decided to send a letter to Mr. Brannock in Georgetown. He wishes to make his and his mother's intentions known once and for all to both of them. They know it will only be a matter of time before he will call on Alice again and they must end any notion of the two marrying. It is best if Mr. Brannock returns, but this time not to the main house, but to The Hermitage. Alice wants only to stay there for the rest of her days and Allard knows this. Once she hears for herself the way of a lumberman's wife's responsibilities, it may persuade her to change her mind regarding Johnathan. And, once Johanthan knows of Alice's affliction, he may not want to be involved with a frail, young girl who will need much medical care.

If this does not convince them both, then the impending engagement to one of the Allston's will have to do. One way or the other, this must end. He sends word to Johnathan to come immediately before they leave for the north. The weather grows more humid by the day and the family wishes to leave soon.

A few days have passed and the family waits for Johnathan's arrival. Alice has been waiting with her Uncle James by the inlet. She is in need of his counsel. Maybe he can help her make her intentions clearer to the family if she has the reverend by her side. She has a deep feeling that this meeting isn't about learning more about Johnathan but to find a way to separate the two, forever.

James places his arm around her shoulder and notices the serious look upon her face. She confides to him in confidence of the initial meeting between Johnathan and herself in Charleston and the letters they wrote to each other. She can nearly recite them word for word and her voice lightens as she speaks his name. James watches her face beam with excitement when she speaks of Johnathan's kind, genteel nature. She confides with him the love she feels and the dreams she has of marrying a self made, hard working man like Johnathan. She gives every detail she can to James to create the best impression of her suitor. After Alice has finished her lecture, James finally has a chance to ask a question.

"My lovely niece, you are so full of hope and promise. I see in your eyes and in the lilt of your voice how much he means to you. But, do you also understand that you may not be living here in Murrells Inlet? What if he decides to take you with him, whether it be the next county or state? Have ye thought of this, my child?"

Alice had heard this before from Allard. She was quite sure that if she explained her love and passion for the inlet that Johnathan would never take her away from her precious Hermitage. She could stay there while he traveled and it would not be such a burden. Or,maybe, he could send someone else to manage the business affairs and they could stay on the inlet together.

James lightly laughs at Alice's naivete. He explains to her that if Johnathan's work takes him elsewhere, such as North Carolina or Georgia, that she will need to follow. She must listen to her husband's bidding. But, Alice believes she can talk Johnathan into staying at Hermitage.

James folds his hands and says a small prayer. This, he believes, is all he can do at this time. The decision is up to his sister and nephew.

Both James and Alice look up towards the house and see Sista running down the embankment towards the creek. She tells Alice she is wanted at the house.

"Oh, please Uncle...is there anything more you can do?"

"My dear, it is in God's hands, now."

Alice makes her way back to the Hermitage. She is both excited and anxious about this meeting. As she turns the corner, she sees Johnathan riding towards the house. His tall, thin stature upon his horse makes him look imposing. Allard has already summoned Hurricane to hitch the horses to his carriage.

"Where are you going, brother?"she asks.

"WE are going for a leisurely tour around the property. I wish to show Mr. Brannock our estate and discuss the matter at hand."

"And, that matter being?"

"Your future, my dear."

Johnathan reaches the side of the carriage and begins to dismount. Allard stops him and communicates his plans for the three of them.

"Mr. Brannock, I hope you had a pleasant journey. Welcome to the Hermitage. As you can see it is still in construction. I had hoped you would ride along with my sister and myself as we explore the surroundings."

"Good day, Dr. Flagg. I would very much enjoy seeing the progress of this beautiful home. Alice has described it to me many times. It is a breathtaking area indeed for a family dwelling."

Alice steps into the carriage to the left of her brother. Jonathan begins to swing his horse around to her side of the carriage, but Allard stops him.

"No, my boy, please stay to my right. I wish to have a discussion with you and do not wish to raise my voice over the sound of the carriage wheels."

Allard has now positioned himself between Alice and Johnathan. He has Hurricane direct the horses towards the south of the property first.

"I have heard you speak, Mr. Brannock, of your father's business and wish to learn more. I understand the concept behind procuring the pitch from our beautiful pines, but I am also aware that you must travel quite often to manage his affairs, correct?"

"Yes, it is a necessary requirement to manage the workers on occasion at each location. Just as you must have an overseer for your plantation and you on occasion must oversee his affairs."

"But, my boy, you must leave the county and sometimes the state for many days, if not weeks, true?"

Alice can tell where the conversation is heading. She does not wish to answer for Johnathan, but has to step in.

"Brother, I know how much time Johnathan must spend at his properties, but he will always come back to me here at the Hermitage."

Allard is about to switch the topic, for he can see Johnathan smile at Alice as she made her remark.

"And, of course, it would be terrible if you were to be away during a time when Alice would need you most. For instance, when she circums to one of her many spells."

Johnathan looks puzzled and turns towards Alice. Her face becomes flushed and she quickly looks down.

"Yes, you see, she is quite frail due to a breathing problem she has had since childhood. It takes quite a lot to bring her back to health. I am here to administer to my family, however at times, I must leave on business as well. I would feel such guilt if I were not by my sister's side when she needed me most. Would you not feel the same?"

Johnathan is silent for a moment. He is trying to find the right words, but he falls short of an answer.

"It seems", continues Allard, "that Mr. Joseph P. Allston of Waverly Plantation is a fine choice for my sister. He and Alice would create a great acquisition for both the Allstons and Flaggs. He and his family have a rather extensive portfolio and Alice will want for nothing. He advises me that he will take great care of Alice and I have accepted his proposal."

Alice is appalled at her brother's cold-hearted approach. She has never seen such provocation nor could she imagine such a savage tactic to end her relationship.

It was with that last statement that Johnathan stopped his horse. But, the carriage continues to move forward. Hurricane turns around to see if he should halt, but Allard points forward with his riding crop and the buggy continues down the avenue. Alice turns around and is saddened to see Johnathan now heading north. She reaches her hand out and cries "Johnathan!" But he does not look back.

Back at the Hermitage, Alice jumps from the buggy. She falls and lands on her hands and knees, her dress caught in the wheel well. Allard's wife Penelope walks towards her and tries to assist, but Alice pulls away.

"Leave me be. I have no quarrel with you, sister-in-law, but I can not think you did not know of my brother's scheme."

"Scheme? What has happened?" Penelope turns towards Allard for an answer.

"Dear wife, do not trouble yourself. This pertains to Mrs. Flagg and myself."

"I am Mrs. Flagg and I would think it would be my place to help my sister-in-law in her hour of need."

Allard allows Penelope to take Alice inside. The entire household echoes with the cries from Alice. She is inconsolable. She has not felt such pain even since the death of her father. This is a new, altogether different pain. Not only the pain of lost love, but the pain of deception. Her breathing becomes labored. She is unable to stop hyperventilating. She feels herself go limp and falls to the ground.

"Allard, come quickly!" cries out Penelope.

Allard rushes in and finds Alice unconscious on the hallway floor. He swiftly picks her up in his arms and carries her to a sofa in the parlor.

"My bag...retrieve my bag!"

A servant runs to find the doctor's bag while Penelope rushes to draw water from a pitcher.

Penelope can hear Allard just under his breath mutter,"None of this would happen if not for that Mr. Brannock."

Margaret has heard the commotion and runs to the parlor. She kneels beside the sofa and strokes Alice's hair. Allard lightly taps Alice's hand in an attempt to wake her. She begins to open her eyes, still having some trouble catching her breath. The pink of her cheeks has come back and she takes a couple of deep breaths. Once she sees Allard, she pulls her hand away.

"Leave me be. I wish not to see nor talk to you." She gazes at her mother's face and begins to cry again.

"Let us take her upstairs and leave her be. It will now be up to time to heal her heart, not us."

A servant brings the doctor's bag and he carries Alice up to her room. There is still a cloudiness to the air from the carpenter's sawdust and the windows must be kept open so Alice can catch her breath. The air is becoming steamy. Summer will be arriving soon and it will be time for the family to go north.

The next several days Alice refuses to leave her room. She is not eating except when Sista begs her to try just a mouthful of rice. Sista is the only person Alice is engaging with. Even her Uncle James has tried to talk to her, but she felt her message regarding her future with Johnathan had fallen on deaf ears. She can trust no one. Only Sista. When the family comes back from the north, Alice will be sent back to school and the Allstons and Flaggs will begin making arrangements for her new life. By the winter solstice, it would become official. Alice and Joseph must begin a future.

Chapter Eight

Fall arrived and the majority of plantations had good crop yields. Harvesting has been steady and the Flagg's are extremely happy with the figures for the year so far. Alice has just turned 15 and is back for her last semester at school before she returns to Murrells Inlet. She has been very melancholy the past few months and does not associate with any of the other students. She attends her classes in music and writing and when Miss Murden dismisses them, she heads to her room. This is how she fills her days during the autumn months until the cold of winter arrives.

But, a very special event will arrive this winter. It is the St. Cecelia's Ball. This is an auspicious occasion for all young girls Alice's age to be introduced into proper society. The cotillion will be for the most elite families of Charleston. Men dressed in their white ties and tails and young ladies in beautiful white gowns. Once the cotillion is over, Alice's engagement to Joseph Allston can be announced. It will be an exciting time for all...except for Alice. She has resigned herself to the fact that she must prepare for a life of long, lonely days with Joseph in Charleston. Joseph owns plantations from Murrells Inlet to Charleston, but he prefers to stay in the city. And so must she. During her time at school, Allard and Penelope are preparing for life in the Hermitage. Penelope is hoping for a child by next summer. Her Uncle James has his mission work and brother Arthur has completed medical school and is enjoying his time in Charleston. Everyone is enjoying life. Everyone...except Alice.

The young ladies at her school talk of nothing but the cotillion. They are having their gowns handmade from the most beautiful satins and silks. This is the most important day in their lives...at least until their wedding day. But to many this is the chance of a lifetime to meet the man they wish to wed. Alice is not very excited about her gown. She has little to say in the matter. Margaret has taken the opportunity to have one created for her. It seems Alice has little say in regards to her life anymore. Her life has been spelled out for her.

Not only will Alice be living in Charleston with Joseph, Margaret will be there a good deal of the time as well. She prefers the city to the country and looks forward to spending her days with Alice in her palatial estate. She can leave the plantation finances up to Allard now and enjoy a life of leisure. Oh, her hand will still be in his pocket quite deep. Her name is still on the deed and she does own the majority of the slaves on Wachesaw. But she has raised her son well. He is content with his livelihood, his wife and his practice. Margaret has done her job and she has done it well.

Alice is to go to Georgetown to meet the seamstress who is creating her gown. Margaret sends her the address along with enough funds to finish the dress. She has given the seamstress strict instructions on the design of the gown. Alice is to go for a final fitting and head back to Charleston. Alice reluctantly heads to Georgetown with Sista by her side. It seems no matter what Sista says to Alice, it does not seem to help her cause. It is as though all the color has drained from her life.

There are few words said along the ride to Georgetown. Alice stares out the window of the carriage and sees that familiar harbor. Her heart skips a beat. She wonders if, just if, she may see him again. How would he react? How would she? She would not know until they met face to face: his blue eyes to her brown eyes.

The carriage stops at the agreed upon location and Alice exits the buggy. She takes a moment to look along the harbor. It is a busy time in Georgetown due to the recent harvests and there is much noise and people along the streets.

She looks among the crowds but can not see beyond the square. She enters the building and hands over the instructions for her gown.

The seamstress brings out the gown and helps Alice into it. Once it is adjusted a little, she looks into a mirror. For a moment, Alice smiles. She imagines that this is her wedding gown and Johnathan is by her side. But, within a minute she remembers her mission. She hangs her head and asks the woman to remove the gown. She helps her undress and Alice quickly puts on her calico dress. She tells the seamstress the dress will work just fine and pays her. She will take the dress as is. The seamstress says she only has a few more fittings to sew on the dress, but Alice does not fret over it. She does not want to put the dress on until the day of the cotillion. She is not looking forward to attending the event.

Alice walks out the door of the building and hands the dress to Sista. Sista's eyes light up when she sees this beautiful gown.

"Ya's gonna be the mos' bu-te-ful girl at de pawty."

"It will not matter. The only person I wish to see me in this gown will not be attending."

Both girls walk towards the carriage. A sudden breeze nearly blows the gown out of Sista's hands. As both girls reach for the gown, another hand quickly swoops in and catches hold of it. Alice hears a man's voice.

"My humblest apologies...I hope I have not caused damage to your dress."

Alice twirls around with a smile on her face. But, all she sees is a kind, older gentleman. It is not who she thought it was. She takes the gown from his arms and quietly thanks him. Sista and she go back to the buggy and head for Charleston.

The trip back to school seems even longer than before. The weather has become chilly and misty on the road to Charleston. Finally, that evening, they reached the school. Sista helps Alice with her gown and follows her up the stairs. Both girls are quite exhausted and Sista helps

Alice put on her bedclothes. Sista leaves the room and heads towards the slave quarters.

Sista is quite sad at the turn of events for her friend. She only wishes she could help in some way. She had one option. Although she knew she could get into terrible trouble for what she was about to do, she was only thinking of Alice. Maybe this one selfless act could help her friend. But, if she is caught, there is no telling what punishment lies ahead. Should she take the chance?

The following day is an important one. The St. Cecilia's Ball. It is all the students at the school are talking about. The event starts late in the evening and the main course is not served until midnight. But, it will take all day for the ladies to prepare. There is an air of excitement for everyone but Alice. She wakes up to see the dreary weather has not improved since the day before. Just looking at the cloudy sky makes her more depressed. She takes in a deep breath, but begins to cough. Her chest is tight and she has trouble clearing her throat. But, she has gone through this many times before and is not concerned. Her medicine is in her bureau but she does not take a drop. She has lost hope and does not try to relieve her ailment.

Sista knocks and then enters Alice's room. Alice is quiet but tries to put a smile on her face for Sista. They spend the rest of the day preparing for this grand party. Once Alice slips on her dress, she is taken back by how pale she looks in the white fabric. Sista notices this too and asks if she is feeling well. Alice quietly answers yes and they continue to get ready.

Alice sees herself in her gown. Turning to Sista, she says she does not wish to go and begins to cry. Sista hands a handkerchief to Alice.

"Please, my sista,'ya mus go. Don cry. I pray ta de Lawd fer ya. He make ev'ryting awright. Ya' see." Sista dries Alice's face and continues to brush her hair. "Ev'ryting be awright."

The time has come to go to the ball and Margaret has arrived to ensure that her daughter's prepared. She walks into the school parlor and finds Alice in her snow white gown, her auburn hair in french curls draping her face. She has Alice turn around so she can inspect the gown. She is surprised the fit isn't as tight as she had thought it should be, but assumes Alice had lost a little weight in recent weeks due to her rigid school activities.

"My child, you look absolutely stunning! This will surely be a night to remember. Are you excited for your debut?"

"Yes, mother."Alice quietly answers, no clear expression of enthusiasm in her voice nor on her face.

"Well, let us join the others. Your brother, Arthur will be there as well. It will be a joyous occasion for the family."

The ladies reach the landing and watch the other young girls rush to their carriages. The clatter of horses hooves and carriage wheels gives the air of an endless parade over the cobblestones street. One by one,they make their way to the South Carolina Society Hall on Meeting Street. Gentlemen greet each carriage and assist the young ladies to the hall. A grand portico overwhelms the entrance of the building. There are quite a few debutantes at this year's event. And the list is that of the most elite.

A young man walks towards Margaret's and Alice's carriage. It is Joseph Allston. He is three years older than Alice, but looks much more mature for his age. His hair is already receding and he has put on much weight since Alice had last seen him. He gives a warm welcome and takes hold of Margaret's hand first. He helps her out of the carriage. Her son Arthur arrives at the same time and takes his mother by the arm and escorts her to the entrance. Joseph reaches his white gloved hand towards Alice. She does not move.

"Miss Flagg, it is time. Won't you please let me escort you?"

Alice finally reaches out her hand and takes his. She turns her head and coughs, excusing herself.

Joseph asks if she is alright. Alice nods and takes his arm. This is an overwhelming event for her and she is already feeling faint by it all. She assumes she is just overcome with nerves and walks into the grand hall.

The sights and sounds of the cotillion are saturating. The music is quite loud so guests must raise their voices to be heard. The young people are dancing in perfect rhythm to the orchestra. White dresses twirl around like snowflakes blowing in the wind. Young gentlemen bowing and escorting their future brides. Families are catching up on local news and showing off the beauty of their daughters.

Alice is completely caught off guard by all the chatter and noise. Her head is spinning and asks Joseph to find a place where she may sit. He honors her request and finds a small sofa. He tells her he will bring her a refreshment and will return momentarily.

Alice feels her chest become tighter. She believes if she goes out for a breath of fresh air she will feel better. She turns to leave through a mahogany door facing the gardens. She is almost to the door, when she suddenly feels her dress snagged on something behind her. She pulls but it does not release. She turns around and hears a voice.

"My humblest apologies...but I believe I have damaged your dress... again."

Alice sees those familiar blue eyes and recognizes the voice. It is Johnathan. A burst of energy enters her and she is filled with warmth and joy. Jonathan takes her by the hand and they make their way outside to the gardens for privacy.

"Johnathan...my Johnathan. I have prayed that you would enter my world again. How did you know I would attend this function?"

"Your partner in crime, Sista. I was quite surprised to see her last evening. She took a risk coming to see me. Had anyone else seen her, her future would not be a happy one."

Alice smiles for the first time in months. Her eyes light up with every word he speaks. They must continue to walk further into the garden to escape the attention of her mother and Joseph. The night air is moist and a gentle fog rolls in over the harbor. Alice is so full of happiness she doesn't mind nor feel the cold mist. All she can think of is her Johnathan.

"My dearest Alice. Can you forgive me?"

"Forgive you? For stepping on my dress?"

"For leaving you. That was a cowardly gesture on my part. I had not handled your brother's interrogation well and I have felt nothing but guilt for not standing up to him. No matter what we face, we will face it together."

Johnathan takes Alice by her left hand,reaches into his coat pocket and pulls out a ring.

"I am here to win your hand. Please, my darling, would you do me the honor of being my wife."

Alice puts both her hands to her mouth as if to pray. She looks at the ring and answers immediately... "Yes."

Johnathan places the ring on her left hand. Alice holds her hand towards the sky. She has never felt so happy. But, she suddenly remembers her whereabouts and looks towards Johnathan.

"How am I to explain this turn of events to my mother, my family? This is neither the time nor place. My love, do not find me uncaring, but I must hide the ring for now. This will cause quite the scandal and we must continue to hide our love, if only for a short while. I do love you. But it is better this way."

Alice slowly takes the ring off her finger. She takes a ribbon off her sleeve and slips the ring upon it. She then ties the ribbon on her neck but keeps the ring below the neckline of her dress.

"I wear this ring by my heart, where it truly belongs."

For the first time, Johnathan and Alice kiss beneath a cold winter's night moon. A gentle rain falls upon them and both run towards the mahogany doors.

"Johnathan, you must go. I will see you again soon, my love. I will leave word in the cemetery wall when we can meet again and we will inform my family of our decision to wed. We shall be together...forever."

Johnathan bows and kisses Alice's hand. He knows this is the best decision. To tell the family here would be an awful mistake. This time, he will not lose her to anyone or anything ever again.

Alice adjusts her ring on the ribbon to make sure it is not seen and enters the hall. Joseph and her mother have been searching for her and were quite upset at her departure.

"Where have you been, child? We searched everywhere for you."

"I felt a little light-headed and needed some air. I am fine now."

Margaret takes a look at Alice and sees her complexion has become quite pale. Joseph takes Alice's hand and asks if she would join him in a dance. She decides it is the best thing to do to cover up her indiscretion and agrees. They take the floor and begin to waltz. The dancing is causing Alice's head to spin, but she is too happy to care. She continues her dance and imagines she is dancing with Johnathan. She smiles and dances until the cotillion is over.

The ball has continued until the wee hours of the morning. Alice and Joseph say their farewells by her carriage. Joseph takes Alice's hand in his and kisses it. She instinctively pulls away. She suddenly realizes what she has done and offers her hand again. She must play this role of future wife just a little while longer until she and Johnathan can confront her family once and for all.

Her carriage pulls away and she is free. Free of the lies and free to be with Johnathan. As she rides away she grows increasingly more tired. She has been invited to stay the night at Arthur's home and hopefully may stay longer. This will give her more time to spend with Johnathan and they can prepare their next move.

The following day, Margaret must leave Charleston. She has been invited to spend time with the Alston family up north so they may make arrangements for the marriage. Margaret says her farewell to her daughter at Arthur's home. She is too excited regarding the wedding arrangements to see that Alice's face has become more ashen in color.

Alice is excited to stay at her brother Arthur's home while Margaret is away. She finds this the perfect place to continue her rendezvous with Johnathan. Her confidante Sista is still by her side. She is the only one who knows Alice's secret.

Chapter Nine

Arthur is already at breakfast in his dining room. He is growing impatient. Alice has not been down to join him and he does not like to wait. He asks one of his servants to fetch her. A few minutes later, the servant rushes down the steps. She exclaims that Alice is not well and to come quickly. He grabs his bag and heads to her bedroom.

The guest room is silent. Alice lies motionless on her bed. Beads of sweat around her brow. It is that moment that Sista walks into the room, unaware of her friend's predicament.

Arthur is stunned. He has only just recently left medical school and has not worked with many patients, let alone his only sister. He seems to panic. Clearing his head, he approaches her and feels for a pulse. It is shallow but there. He places his ear to her chest and listens to her heart. It beats in a slow, methodical rhythm. He knows quite well of Alice's health problems and reaches for the first thing he can think of...opium and mercury. He knew Alice was used to taking small doses of opium for her asthma and quickly thought to prescribe a dose. Mercury had not been used before to treat her breathing but he knew from his studies that it was important to release bodily fluids to rid infection. This was a well-known remedy among doctors of the time. He would also try mustard packs to ease her suffering.

Arthur tries to wake Alice and she opens her eyes slowly.

"My dear, are you in any pain?"

Alice points to her ribcage area. Arthur listens again to her breathing.

" Your breathing sounds labored so I advise a dose of your opium to begin. We will see how you feel and continue with mercury next."

Sista walks quietly towards Alice's bed. A tear falls from her eye and down her cheek. Alice gives a tiny grin and reaches up to wipe it away.

"Sista, my sista, do not despair. I will be right as rain. You'll see."

Arthur gives a small dose of opium to Alice. He instructs the servants to watch over her. If the opium doesn't soothe her symptoms, he will have to use cupping or mustard packs to increase her lung capacity. But for now, he sees this as another 'spell' and tells the others to let her rest. Arthur returns downstairs and leaves for the day. He has another patient to follow up with across town. He informs a servant he will be back later that afternoon and to prepare another room for his brother Dr. Allard. He is expecting his brother to visit within the day and hopes Alice is in better health before he arrives.

Sista can not leave Alice's side. She knows this is more serious than other attacks from the past. However, she knows her place and can't argue with the doctor. All she can do is sit and watch over her sweet Alice.

She whispers to Alice if there is anything she can do for her. Maybe, send a note to Johnathan regarding her health.

"No...he must not see me like this. I do not wish to burden him or make known to my family of our future plans. Promise me you will not tell him. I will regain my strength. I have much to look forward to...see. I am to be Mrs. Johnathan Brannock." Alice uncovers the ribbon from her neck and reveals the ring to Sista. She clutches the ring in her hand as if it were a talisman. She believes this is all she will need to regain her health.

Minutes feel like hours to Sista. Alice's breathing has become much worse. There is a terrible wheezing as she struggles to take each breath. Sista goes to one of the servants and asks where Arthur is. They do not know his exact whereabouts and Sista becomes concerned. She is nervous to give another dose of opium. She feels it has only made the condition worse. She runs back to Alice's side and watches her dearest friend fade away.

"Pease, Lawd, she too young. Dun take 'er."

Alice looks up at Sista's face. Alice's face is grey and her eyes are dilated. She gives Sista a faint smile and takes one more breath. This time ,however, the wheezing stops. Alice becomes limp and Sista waits anxiously for Alice to take another breath but she is quiet. Her eyes slowly close. One last tear falls down her cheek. Alice's hand opens and reveals her ring. Sista knows she has one more favor to do for her friend. Sista takes the ring and hides it under Alice's dress collar. She lightly strokes Alice's face and hair, falls to her knees and weeps.

Sista has no idea how long she has been by Alice's side. She knows she must find someone to help. She rises off the bedroom floor and makes her way downstairs. She walks threw the front door in a state of shock and into the courtyard. Arthur is just arriving home and sees Sista standing alone in the front yard staring into the sky.

"Girl, why are you not with my sister?"

Sista slowly brings her gaze down. Arthur can tell what has just happened by the expression on Sista's face. He pushes her aside and runs into the home. He bounds up the stairs and pushes the bedroom door open. He sees his sister lying on the bed, a calm peaceful look across her face. He rushes to her and opens her eyes. They are fixed and without life. He feels for a pulse over and over, but there is none that he can find. He collapses on the floor and is stunned. '*This cannot be...this cannot be!*' After several minutes, he stands and takes the sheet from the bed and covers his sister. He sits at the bottom of the bed shaking his head in disbelief. All he can do now is wait for his brother, Allard, to arrive and tell him the heartbreaking news.

It is near nightfall when Allard's carriage is heard coming down the alley. Sista is still outside, not quite sure what to do with herself. She has just lost the only person who treated her like a true friend. It isn't until the sound of horses approaching that she turns to look. She sees her father, Hurricane, driving a carriage towards her. She knows it's Dr. Allard arriving. She rushes towards her father. He abruptly stops and jumps off the carriage to open Allard's door, all the while looking at Sista. Allard steps down and notices the look on Sista's face.

"Sista, I know you are not here to greet me ... give your father time to finish his duty before you say your hello." Allard watches Sista run into Hurricane's arms. Hurricane is embarrassed and alarmed by this but within seconds realizes something is terribly wrong. Allard walks towards the front door and before he can knock is met by Arthur. He has a look of complete failure on his face.

"Brother, what has happened?"

Arthur can only shake his head, unable to speak.

Allard repeats his question and receives an answer, "I tried...I tried, but she is gone."

Allard gives a look of confusion. "Whom are you speaking of?!"

Arthur's voice shakes as he answers..."Alice."

Allard quickly rushes to the second floor, running from one room to the next searching for his sister. He reaches her room and finds his sister lying beneath a white sheet. He slowly reaches out but is unable to pull the sheet away to look upon his sister's face. He can not believe what he is witnessing. His instinct as a doctor is not present. Only a broken hearted brother stands alone in the room. He approaches to pull the sheet again, but can not. He retreats downstairs to question Arthur.

The two brothers both question and console each other. Arthur can not understand what has gone wrong. Alice had spells before and always revived. But, it was worse than anyone had imagined.

Allard decides that he and Arthur must take Alice home. They will send word to their mother and decide on burial arrangements once they are reunited in Murrells Inlet. This will be the hardest letter either has written. They instruct Sista to pack Alice's clothing, including the white gown she wore at the cotillion. The other servants perform their duties somberly. It is a cold, January day not only outside but within the house as well. The two brothers ready themselves for the trip to the inlet.

Hurricane sits with his daughter in the servants quarters attempting to eat his supper, but he, too, is devastated by the news of Alice's death. He reaches out to take Sista's hand.

"Ya' awright?"

Sista doesn't know how to answer. She still does not want to believe what has happened. She releases her hand from her father's grasp and walks away. She knows she must go upstairs to pack Alice's belongings for the journey home.

Arthur has packed his carriage with all they will need for the ride back to Wachesaw Plantation. Allard will take Alice with him. The journey starts just before daybreak. Sista will ride on the front of the carriage with her father, both wrapped up warm and tight. Allard has instructed that they move quickly before any bad weather approaches. They will travel non stop until they reach home.

Hours have passed and the road has become more uneven. The mud has hardened and it has been a rough ride for all. They turn the corner a few miles from their home when Allard's carriage hits a large stone in the road. The carriage shifts harshly. It is then that Allard hears something. He hears a gasp. A faint gasp. He pauses a minute and hears it again. And again. He is astonished! He reaches towards his sister and there is movement beneath the blankets.

"Alice...Alice can you hear me?" He reaches for her hand. Her tiny fingers move.

'Dearest God in Heaven...she's alive!'

Allard begins to bang on the carriage roof, yelling instructions to Hurricane to move faster. They must get to the house quickly.

Allard holds his sister tight.

"Alice, my darling sister, we are almost home. Do not worry for I am here."

Alice tries desperately to speak. She can only call out one word ... "*Hermitage*".

"My dear, we must get you to the main house."

"Hermitage."

Allard understands that she has not much time left and so he decides to fulfill what may be her last request. Allard again beats on the carriage wall and yells to Hurricane to take them to the Hermitage.

Hurricane and Sista cannot understand why they must rush but do as instructed. Hurricane snaps the horses reins and they gallop as fast as conditions allow. Arthur's carriage was following behind. He does not understand why Allard's carriage is traveling so fast. He instructs his servant to hurry as well. After a few miles, he realizes Allard is heading to the Hermitage.

Allard takes hold of his sister. She is cold to the touch but still breathing slowly. She tries to hug him but has no energy in her. She whispers the word '*Hermitage*' over and over.

"We are nearly there,sweet girl. We are nearly there."

The carriage comes to a stop at the Hermitage. Allard jumps out of the carriage with Alice wrapped tight in his arms. He flies up the porch steps and forces his way through the door. He ascends the staircase and places his sister in bed. He cries out to the servants to light the fireplace and retrieve his bag from the coach. He belts out one command after the other. Arthur's carriage has pulled up and he leaps out, hurrying up the stairs.

Once he reaches Alice's bedroom, Arthur shrieks, "What in God's name has possessed you to come here?"

Allard steps aside and shows him the reason, pointing at Alice on the bed. Alice opens her eyes. Arthur is in shock.

"What has happened...is she breathing? How is this possible?"

"She was comatose, I believe." Allard bends over to listen to Alice's lungs. "She is filled with fluid...pneumonia."

Allard is upset with his brother but not harsh. This is not the time to berate him for his diagnosis. He has seen this before. He had heard of patients being misdiagnosed, barely conscious and some buried alive. But, now, the most important thing is to keep Alice warm and guide her back to health.

The two brothers spend hours by her side. They had already sent word to their mother, however she will think they are at the main house. It will take days before she will be back home. They still haven't written to brother Eben to inform him of this turn of events. The household is whirling with sadness and fear.

Sista is both elated but cautious at hearing the news. She sits on the floor at the side of Alice's bed, praying that she not leave her once again.

Dr. Allard enters the room and feels for Alice's pulse on her neck. A pale blue ribbon blocks his way. He unties it and as he lifts it away, he hears the sound of metal falling. He looks towards the floor and sees the ring. He slowly picks it up, examining it.

He turns to Sista, still sitting on the floor.

"Girl, what is this I have found with my sister?"Sista is afraid to answer. She quickly shakes her head.

"Girl, I will not ask this of you again. Where has this come from?"

Sista lowers her head. She does not want to betray her sister, her friend.

A whisper comes from behind Allard.

"My ring."

He turns around and sees Alice reach up towards him.

"My ring...where is my ring?"

Allard has deduced whose ring it is. Clutching the ring in his hand, he mutters the name, "Brannock."

He takes another look at Sista. She is still on the floor with her head bent low.

"This is Brannock's, isn't it? Did he meet with her in Charleston?"

"Brother, please, give me my ring. Leave her be"

Allard turns to Alice. Her voice is low and soft, "I love Johnathan. I ...love...him. Please...my ring." Alice's eyes roll back, then close.

Allard is extremely alarmed to find that the two had gone behind his and his mother's backs. He walks out of the room, down the stairs and outside. He becomes more furious with each step. He continues to march towards the marsh. Once there, his anger mounts. He opens his clenched hand and finds he still has Alice's ring. It has etched a perfectly round imprint in his hand. He believes Johnathan is the reason his little sister is ill and dying. He takes the ring and throws it into the marsh. The very moment the ring leaves his grasp, he realizes what he has just done, but it is too late. He watches as the ring sparkles in the sunlight and then is lost in the marshy pluff mud.

Allard's anger has turned to shame. He has tossed away his sister's reason for living. He walks slowly back towards the house to care for Alice. Once there, he notices her breathing is worse. She tries to speak but only coughs violently. She is struggling more and more.

She looks into Allards eyes. "My ring?"

He bows his head and tells her all will be well. He does not mention the fate of her ring.

Throughout the day, Alice continues to murmur the words *'my ring'* over and over. Allard is terribly distraught at what he has done. He calls to his servants and tells them to search the marsh for a small gold ring. The slaves look puzzled at each other. They know they will not be able to find a ring in this huge body of water and mud. They do as instructed and head into the cold waterway. They spend hours searching but no one is able to discover Alice's ring. Hurricane is also helping with the search. But when darkness comes, they must end their mission.

Hurricane drags himself into the home. Sista and Martha huddle together in the kitchen with tears in their eyes.

Hurricane looks at Sista and asks if she knows why they are sent out in the freezing water to search for a ring? Sista can not confide everything she knows regarding Johnathan and Alice to them. She can only tell them that the ring meant everything to Alice. Hurricane demands to know what happened when they were in Charleston. Sista can not lie to her father. She tells of Alice's love for Johnathan, that the ring is from him and about the letters she delivered for them.

"Ya' hep her? Why? Ya' know we be in big trouble if'n theys find out. Doc Allard hep us. He a good man...he fix ma' hand! Ya' knew she not s'pose to have nuthin' to do with Mr Brannock. If'n he find out, we be done."

Sista looks towards Martha. Martha takes hold of her husband's left hand and whispers, "Well ten, he ain't neva' gonna find out."

Allard decides he must confide in his brother and Uncle James about Alice's ring. James is quite upset with Allard's impulsive reaction with the ring. He reprimands Allard , but knows that will not solve the problem. James goes to his home and remembers he still has his first wife's ring. He goes to his desk and opens the drawer. There it is. He sits and remembers fondly of his first love. Her fingers were so slim her ring would fall off. How many times they would be searching under cabinets and tables for her ring. How many times they laughed throughout the years. Those very few years. She passed away all too soon from the spread of yellow fever that had taken over the area a decade ago. He understands what Alice wants. She wants that carefree, simple kind of love. Not huge mansions. Not acre upon acre of rice and cotton plantations. She simply wants love. Pure and sweet. There was that type of love. He remembered it. He experienced it himself.

James returns to Hermitage with his ring. He tells Allard it is his duty to give the ring to Alice. Allard takes it upstairs. Alice is struggling for breath. He takes her hand and places the ring in her palm. She slowly closes her hand. Without even looking, she immediately drops the ring to the floor.

"I want MY ring. Where is MY ring?"

Allard bends down and picks up the ring. He turns towards his little sister. And with those final words, she is gone.

Allard again listens to her heart, her chest and takes her pulse. He brings a mirror to her lips, hoping her breath will cloud it. He sits for minutes, staring at the mirror. It remains the same.

He raises up from her bed and heads towards the hall. He stands at the landing looking down at his family. Arthur and James are there along with the house servants. With their own eyes they can see that he is defeated. James slowly marches upstairs. He must offer up a final prayer for Alice. They could not save her body, but he will be there to release her soul.

The family now faces the daunting task of preparing for Margaret's arrival. Arrangements for Alice can not be made until she returns. Eben Jr. has finally arrived and sits with his brothers awaiting their mother's return. This would be the most heartbreaking experience of all.

It had only been a few months since Margaret buried her father and is now still in mourning over the loss. Margaret has resigned herself to wearing black year after year. None of the brothers can remember the last time she had worn a brightly colored gown or not worn a veil across her face. They knew the news of Alice's passing might be too much for their mother to bear.

It would be twilight when the three brothers hear a familiar voice entering the main hall. Margaret is worn and looks puzzled. She approaches Allard and asks "Why are you not at the main house? Why has everyone assembled here? And where is Alice...upstairs?" Margaret begins to go up but Allard takes her by the arm.

"Mother, I, I mean... we have disheartening news."

"Allard why do you keep me from my child?"

"Please sit, mother."

Margaret looks first at Allard, then Arthur and Eben. The looks on their faces are obvious. She has never seen all three with tears in their eyes. She pulls her arm away from Allard's grasp and walks upstairs.

Margaret enters the bedroom. There is no fire in the fireplace but there are candles lit all around the room. Her body casts a black shadow across the bed. A black linen sheet is placed across the mattress. An outline of a person lies beneath.

Margaret is unable to move. She stands motionless, candles flickering all around her.

A moment later, the brothers hear their mother cry out a single word... 'NO!' She walks out onto the landing and shouts, "Where is my daughter?"

Arthur answers,"Mother, I am so sorry. Alice has passed away."

"No, no, that is not her. Where is my daughter? She is not beneath that linen. Give me my child!"

All three walk up the stairs. Margaret begins to cry. The closer they come to her, the more she believes that Alice is dead. Allard reaches out to hold his mother, but she pulls away and turns back into the room.

"This can not be. I can not bury another child. I can not. You are all doctors. Do what you have been trained to do. Bring me back my daughter!"

All three men stand without a word in the hall. Margaret takes a deep breath and inches her way back to the bed. She takes hold of the black crepe fabric and pulls it away carefully. A white, pale face draped with long auburn hair is illuminated by the candle light. There is no denying it now. She has lost her treasure...her baby, her last little girl. The one she sought to protect. She had failed. Her hopes and dreams were lying there within a cold, darkened room.

Allard and Arthur enter. They take the drape and replace it over Alice's face and walk Margaret to the parlor. Once there, they offer her a sherry and help her to the sofa.

"How?"

"Pneumonia."

"When?"

" Two days ago."

"It's my fault." replies Margaret. "Mine. I should not have left her alone. Ever."

Arthur speaks up, " No mother, it is mine. The fault is all mine."

Allard looks to his brother. "No, Arthur, neither you nor mother should condemn yourselves. Had it not been for Mr. Brannock, this would not be."

Eben asks if this is the correct time to bring up the subject of Johnathan.

"Johnathan Brannock? I thought that issue was dealt with. What knowledge do you have regarding Alice and he?"

Allard explains finding the ring around Alice's neck. How they were seeing each other against their wishes and that she had whispered his name before she passed. Margaret takes her glass of sherry and smashes the glass on the ground.

"He has taken my daughter from me forever. For this, I shall never forgive him. He will never be near my sweet Alice ever again."

The ground is frozen solid this January. It will take some time before the family can bury Alice properly. They agree it is best to keep Alice in a shallow root cellar facing the marsh until weather conditions improve. The question lies where her final resting place will be. Margaret knows if word reaches Johnathan of Alice's death, he will look for her at All Saints Cemetery in the family plot. So to keep him away from her child, she will place a memorial stone to Alice there. But, Alice shall actually be buried with her two brothers, Allard Jr. and Edward at Cedar Hill on Reverend Belin's property. Margaret will not put a stone on that grave. It will remain unmarked. Only the family will know her true, final resting place. They can now keep Johnathan away from Alice forever, even in death. He will never know where his true love is. Never again will he see the Hermitage or have anything to do with their lovely, beautiful Alice.

Again Margaret must drape everything in the home with black crepe. A black wreath placed on the door and mirrors covered to keep spirits from entering and leaving. Alice is dressed in her beautiful white cotillion gown. A blue ribbon has been placed around her neck but nothing else adorns it. It will take days for neighbors and friends to pay their respects. People of Charleston who already heard of her passing were coming to Wachesaw as well. Then word spread to Georgetown...and to the ears of Johnathan. He would make his way to All Saints Church in Pawleys Island and wander the cemetery, finally coming across a huge marble stone. It has one name on it...Alice. Here he would come every year for the rest of his life on the anniversary of their engagement and place a ring upon the stone. He silently repeats the words he spoke when he asked for Alice's hand that night at the cotillion. And, softly smiles when he hears her voice answer, '*yes*'.

Time would pass and the Hermitage would be completed in all its glory. But, it would not feel like a warm, coastal cottage to the Belin/ Flagg family.The home that was built on ancient Indian burial ground called Wachesaw has lived up to it's name... '*the place of great weeping.*'

Allard and his wife, Penelope would have a daughter several months after Alice's death. They would name their child, Alice. Penelope would pass away in the Hermitage before her 40th birthday. Some say maybe she has also decided to stay at the Hermitage along with her sister-in-law. There would be times when whispers would be heard throughout the home when no one else was near. Even Dr. Allard would see a woman in white walk towards the marsh and suddenly vanish.

Margaret sealed off Alice's room for nearly a decade. She would wear black for the rest of her days. Finally, the day came when she could enter her bedroom again. On occasion, Margaret would sit on the edge of Alice's bed for hours. Other days, she would gaze into her dressing table mirror. She hoped to see her daughter's reflection combing her long auburn hair. In her later years, family and friends would hear Margaret in Alice's room, still talking to Alice as if she were still there.

Margaret would outlast all of her children, except Allard. Her son, Arthur, would be swept away by a terrible sea surge. Her son, Charles, who spent his entire life in the military, would perish on the battlefield at the end of the Civil War. Eben would die from yellow fever. Which left only Allard. He would often wander down to the edge of the property by the inlet marsh where blue heron and egrets would feast on fish and the gentle breeze blows. He was still looking for the lady in white he had seen by the marsh many, many times...his beautiful sister. And, every once in a while as he walked by the water, he would hear a soft, sweet voice whisper... '*where is my ring?*'

About the Author

Christine (Wannop) Vernon grew up in a suburb of Phila, PA. She spent many years studying both fine arts as well as live theater. She moved to South Carolina in 2005 and began investigating the history and legends of the South Strand. She currently sells her original artwork at her home studio and lectures at museums, universities, and local venues. She owns/operates Miss Chris' Inlet Walking Tour-a local ghost and history tour on the Murrells Inlet MarshWalk.

Read more at https://www.facebook.com/inletcottageandwalkingtour.

www.ingramcontent.com/pod-product-compliance
Ingram Content Group UK Ltd.
Pitfield, Milton Keynes, MK11 3LW, UK
UKHW021656190726
13853UKWH00001B/298

9 798201 811617